DREAMERS

*Let me not
    mar that
    perfect dream
by an auroral stain -
but so adjust my daily night
that it will come again.*

- Emily Dickinson

THE

DREAMERS

OF

OURDH

NEW EDITION

Thelbert Dewain Belgard

Great Way Publications
2013

Great Way Publications
Carmine, Texas
WWW.GreatWayPublications.Info

ISBN 978-0615813257

Contents

Chapter 1—In the garden

FOR JUST an instant, everything was clear. Arenh understood it all. He could see the entire planet from here, a tiny green and blue marble of a world, almost lost in the vastness of the blackness around it. Then he woke up with a start as the tones of the garden chime filled the morning air around the upper entrance to the Mountain.

He had spent the night in the stone watchtower at the edge of the terrace. The cot in the tower wasn't as comfortable as his bed in the Carnelian Cavern, but it was adequate. And the view from the watchtower was magnificent in the morning.

He got up and stood at the door of the tower, stretching for a moment as he breathed in the foggy air, heavy with the fragrance of the honeysuckles that covered the fences. His garden bot was already busy watering the supersoy seedlings they had planted the day before.

A red and blue butterfly fluttered across the garden and settled on his shoulder. "*Such a beautiful morning,*" it whispered in his ear.

Arenh failed to suppress his startle response entirely. "A few more years of mind training will help," he thought. It helped also in this case that he recognized the voice. He had grown accustomed to the

Dreamers whispering in his mind, but that was a much different experience from hearing them whisper in his ear.

"Pardon my surprise," Arenh said. "I wasn't expecting a butterfly to talk."

"*What is talk?*" the butterfly asked. "*Just thoughts drifting on waves of air. But thoughts have no need of air, you know.*" It flitted over closer to his ear and whispered more softly. "*Air, in fact, is made of thoughts.*"

"Is that so?" Arenh smiled. "And what then are thoughts made of?"

"*Now there's a real mystery for you,*" the butterfly mused. "*No one knows. But I'd say paying attention is one of the main ingredients, which is something you should practice more. So pay close attention to what I'm going to tell you now. You must remember it all.*"

With that, the butterfly began to fade away until it had vanished completely, but it continued to whisper in Arenh's mind.

Arenh's father, Lord Ivanh, had heard the whispers of the Dreamers, too. "I believe they're transtemporal beings," his father told him once. But in the years since his father's death, Arenh had come to wonder if that were altogether true.

Perhaps it was true that the Dreamers had transcended the world of time. They remained very much interested, nevertheless, in the events of that world. And they could influence the course of events through their mindlink with people like Arenh and his father or by taking on a form like the butterfly or even by means of a piece of stone like the Amulet.

Arenh sometimes thought of the Dreamers as protectors of the Mountain and its inhabitants. At other times, he wondered if what they really protected were their own interests. He had never fully trusted them, though he found it hard not to trust the butterfly.

Arenh had no doubt, in any case, that the interests of the Dreamers often coincided with his own. And that was certainly true in the case of the message the butterfly had whispered in his mind. The Dreamers had foreseen that the valley people would soon launch another assault against the wall of the City below. An attack by the primitive Ourdhu had never warranted a warning from the Dreamers before. The indigenous people of the planet didn't pose a significant threat to the Terran colonists. But then, the warning wasn't really about the Ourdhu.

A BEEP called his attention back to the garden. His garden bot had finished its task. The morning fog had begun to lift, revealing a crimson and purple sky in the east. It would have been a good morning to work in the garden, but the message of the butterfly required a change in plans. Arenh instructed the garden bot to begin planting another row of seedlings and then walked back into the watchtower, moving in that deliberate and almost ceremonious way in which all the Indigo people moved.

He looked for his tunic. He seldom wore a tunic to the garden. Wearing clothes in the fog made as much sense as wearing them in a shower stall. But he always brought his tunic with him. Well— Maybe not always. He wrapped a towel around his waist and tied it like a loincloth. Then he took the Indigo

Cloak from a hook on the wall, swung it over his left shoulder, and fastened it over the right.

Ten years had passed since Arenh had assumed the Cloak as Lord of the Indigo. But in his heart, it was still his father's cloak. The Cloak had passed to Arenh on the day after his 18th birthday, which was also the day after his father died in a coup d'état led by Adhalmar, the Emerald Lord. Arenh had never celebrated his birthday again. It was, instead, a day to remember his father. And a day to remember what Adhalmar had done.

The coup was sparked by a move of the High Council to limit the Emerald Lord's powers as minister for defense. To avoid civil war, King Edmunh, Lord of the Crimson Clan, was forced to accept the three decrees by which Adhalmar abolished the High Council, made himself prime minister in place of Lord Ivanh, and imprisoned Arenh in the Mountain.

Confinement to the Mountain was never in itself a problem for Arenh. "If Mikah were only permitted to visit," he thought, "I would have no need to be any other place than here."

Mikah was the only son of King Edmunh. He had been Arenh's lover and closest friend since their early teens. Such same-sex pairings were common among the young of the colony. Everyone had thought the two young princes made a handsome couple.

Expectations changed, however, a few years down the road. Everyone expected adults to settle down with a person of the opposite sex and have

4

children. The attachments of youth were just a phase, everyone said.

But Arenh was one of those who couldn't switch gears so easily. In that innermost circle of friends to which one only admits a lover, he had never had room for anyone but Mikah. And that was as true now as it was in his teens.

Mikah's innermost circle, on the other hand, had always been somewhat larger than Arenh's, to put it politely. Even so, Arenh had never doubted his friend's loyalty and devotion.

Arenh stood at the open window of the watchtower and looked out over the City on the high plain below. He could see the Crimson Palace where Mikah now ruled—in name, at least, if not in fact.

The Dreamers had whispered the news a few months before that King Edmunh had died. Arenh had felt Mikah's thoughts at the time. Mikah knew that when his father's life had ended, his life as the carefree playboy prince had ended too. He was suddenly Lord of the Crimson Clan and King of all clans. "And all you ever wanted, my love," Arenh thought, "was to have fun."

The last time the two young men had seen each other, they had been standing together outside the Council Chamber when Edmunh emerged flanked by his guards. There were dark blotches on the Crimson Cloak that appeared to be blood. The king rushed past Arenh and Mikah without looking or speaking.

Mikah started to run after his father. But Jonah, Captain of the Crimson Guard, came running out of the Chamber and called him back.

That was the first time Arenh heard the Dreamers. *"The things of time are not what they seem,"* they had whispered in his mind.

Jonah ordered the guardsmen who had followed him out of the Chamber to surround Arenh and Mikah. The guards quickly encircled their captain and the two princes. They knelt with the force fields of their shields deployed and their beam weapons set to kill. Mikah was clearly alarmed. But Arenh was unafraid.

"The king is not harmed, Your Highness," Jonah assured Mikah. Then he turned towards Arenh with a look of pain on his face. "My Lord," he said as he bowed.

Arenh's heart sank. He felt a painful lump in his throat and bit his tongue to stop the tears. He desperately tried to think of some reason—any reason besides the obvious one—for Jonah to address him that way.

"I regret to inform you that your father is dead and that your own life is in danger." Jonah's voice was soft and kind. But in Arenh's mind, he sounded far away. "You must remain with my guards, until we can get you to the safety of the Mountain."

Chapter 2—Sanctuary

THE NEXT day after the assassination of Lord Ivanh, Edmunh himself escorted Arenh to the Mountain. They were surrounded by the most trusted of Jonah's guardsmen. Two members of the Emerald Guard went with them as witnesses— Prince Karl and Count Hugho, the Emerald captain.

When they reached the entrance, Edmunh and Arenh entered the Mountain, leaving the others outside. Arenh's mother, Lady Julia, and Donna, her lady-in-waiting, were standing inside with a squad of Indigo guardsmen in attendance.

Arenh recognized one of the guardsmen as Donna's son Kodhi. His father had been captain of the Indigo Guard, but Arenh had learned from Jonah that Kodhi's father had taken his own life a few hours after Lord Ivanh's death.

Arenh hugged his mother and Donna. He looked at Kodhi and nodded. But when their eyes met, Kodhi looked quickly away.

"Your Majesty," Lady Julia greeted the king. He acknowledged her by taking her hand in his.

"I'm deeply sorry for your loss my dear," the king said, "and for your loss my son," he said to Arenh. "Ivanh was my dearest friend. Adhalmar refused to permit regeneration. He died in my arms."

Lady Julia wiped her eyes, and Donna—who was also in tears—embraced her.

Edmunh asked Kodhi to remove Arenh's chlamys. After Kodhi had done so, Edmunh took the Indigo Cloak from a bag concealed under his own cloak and fastened it around Arenh's shoulders. "Arenh of the Indigo Clan," he said, "in assuming the Cloak of your Clan, you assume authority over its lands and people. Do you swear to rule them with justice and wisdom?"

Arenh dropped to one knee and said, "I do, Your Majesty."

"Rise, Lord Arenh."

When Arenh stood up, Edmunh embraced him and seemed on the verge of tears. But he regained his composure in a moment and told Arenh with an unsteady voice, "I regret to say that I don't have the Amulet. It wasn't on Ivanh's body. And I'm sure that Adhalmar doesn't have it either. I think the Dreamers have reclaimed it." Then he turned quickly, appearing to be overwhelmed again by his emotions, and left without the usual farewells.

After Edmunh left, Hugho closed the door to the lower entrance and summoned two of his guardsmen to install a heavy bolt to lock it. Arenh still remembered the sounds of the door being bolted from the outside. Adhalmar had kept guards posted at the lower entrance ever since to enforce the decree.

Later, when Arenh and his mother were in the privacy of her apartment in the Amethyst Cavern, she told him, "It would be impossible to imprison you anywhere if you had the Amulet."

Arenh kissed her on the forehead. "That's true," he said softly. "But it no longer exists in the world of time and space if the Dreamers have reclaimed it. Of course, it's still possible the Dreamers may give it to me as they did to Father."

But silently he wondered how they would give it to him if they chose him to be its possessor. His father had never told him how he received the Amulet. Lord Ivanh had talked about it only once. They were in the Crimson Palace, standing outside the Chamber of the High Council, when Arenh asked him what it was.

"It's a thought amplifier that's specifically tuned to location, to one's thoughts about where he is in the world of time and space," his father explained. "Time and space are creations of the mind. The mind doesn't arise from the material world. The material world arises from the mind."

In whatever way Lord Ivanh received the Amulet, Arenh knew he received it soon after he had assumed the Cloak. So after several years had passed, Arenh decided the Dreamers had found him unworthy to wear the artifact. For a while, he also thought of himself as unworthy.

But now, ten years after his father's death, Arenh was at peace with himself. "If the Dreamers don't trust me," he thought, "they should know the feeling is mutual."

The entire Indigo Clan had accepted the years of confinement since Lord Ivanh's death as an opportunity to develop greater equanimity, patience, understanding, and other such spiritual assets.

Arenh had seen those years as an opportunity, also, to develop assets of a different sort.

Immediately after assuming the Cloak, he appointed Kodhi as the new captain of the Indigo Guard. The two of them began right away to plan a military buildup.

A few months later, their plans made a sharp turn when Indigo archaeologists dug into a hidden chamber in one of the deep caverns. It was the boneyard for robots that had been discarded by the ancient builders of the Mountain. The machines were all designed to accept the same artificial brain, though only one still had the AI module installed. The engineers who examined the unit concluded that it was activated by a colony of cloned human brain cells housed at its core. The cells had been dead for thousands of years.

After several failed attempts to reactivate the module with living cells from various donors, a team of geneticists and robotics engineers succeeded, using cells that Arenh had donated.

Kodhi and Arenh were present that day when the AI came alive. They noticed a group of geneticists were whispering to each other and looking at the two of them in a strange way. Kodhi walked over to where the group was standing and asked what was going on.

"They say," he told Arenh when he returned, "that your DNA is a nearly perfect match to that of the original cells in the AI unit. They say that's not possible, but it's a fact. They're dumbfounded."

"So am I," Arenh mumbled.

After the AI was activated, the engineers discovered to their amazement that it had a built-in capacity to replicate itself and the various machines in which it was housed. It only needed the raw materials and the command to proceed.

Within a few years, server bots were floating through the corridors of the Mountain, cleaning bots were crawling around the floors of the caverns, and the barracks of the Guard contained more android than human warriors.

At that point, Kodhi was ready for war. "If we move with the setting sun," he told Arenh, "we can occupy the Emerald Palace before morning."

But Arenh forbade it. "I'm sure we can neutralize the entire Emerald Guard within a few hours, as you say," he told his captain. "But I'm afraid that Adhalmar will use his doomsday weapons if we invade the Emerald Sector."

The situation had changed, however, since that conversation took place. The message of the butterfly had changed everything. Arenh considered going straight to the barracks to tell Kodhi about the warning from the Dreamers. But he had no doubt about what Kodhi's advice would be. He decided to tell Kodhi later. Arenh had found that when he saw no way to go forward, the best thing to do was to sit quietly until a way opened. And the best place to do that was in the meditation hall.

Chapter 3—The turning point

THE MORNING fog had completely vanished by the time Arenh left the watchtower. Though large white clouds gave occasional relief from the sun and the distance he had to walk was short, he was glistening with sweat when he arrived at the upper entrance to the Mountain.

As he entered the corridor to the caverns, he felt a feeling of foreboding, as exciting as it was disturbing, that something major was about to happen. He went directly to the zendo and stood before the altar platform.

Standing on the platform was a life-size statue of the Ancient Mother. She was dressed in an indigo robe. In her right hand, she held a sword, symbolic of her defense of the helpless and oppressed. And in her left hand, she held a blue iris—the Indigo symbol of peace.

Arenh sat down on a cushion in front of the altar and listened to the morning chants of the priests beginning behind him.

And here see form as void
and void as form
and form apart from voidness not
and voidness not apart from form.

The chant was from an ancient Zen scripture of Old Earth. It was chanted over and over in a monotone, very slowly at first and then gradually faster with each repetition. The rhythm was marked by the beat of drums.

Arenh let the words of the chant flow through his mind like water, with no effort to comprehend their meaning. The chant continued until its tempo was furious and the words could hardly be distinguished. And then the chanting came to an abrupt end with a rolling crash of the drums and a deep sonorous bong of the zendo bell.

After the chant ended and the reverberations of the bell faded, Arenh continued to sit for a few moments in the utter silence of the great hall. Then as he brought his palms together and prepared to stand up, he saw something lying on the altar platform that hadn't been there before—a simple necklace of tiny gold links from which was suspended a disk of gold. And on the disk was mounted a small dark blue oval stone.

Arenh took a deep breath and felt his heart begin to pound. They had found him worthy. He felt a moment of guilt for his mistrust of the Dreamers. But then he thought, "Just because they find me worthy of their Amulet doesn't mean I find them worthy of my trust."

He carefully picked up the Amulet and put it over his head so that the stone hung in the center of his chest. When the stone touched his body, he experienced a feeling of déjà vu as the Dreamers whispered in his mind.

*"What is past remains even now,
and what is yet to come is already here.
The things of time are not what they seem.
Hold fast to your faith,
O Dreamer of the Dream.
Do not surrender to your fear."*

Feelings surged through his mind of joy mixed with anxiety and anticipation mixed with dread. He breathed the feelings in and breathed them out until at last he felt at peace.

"I must tell Mother I've found the Amulet," he thought, "but first I must use it to warn Mikah."

Chapter 4—Mikah

ARENH focused his attention on a memory of Mikah's apartment in the Crimson Palace. He had been there many years before. Then he pressed the Amulet to his chest while he breathed out and closed his eyes. He breathed in and opened his eyes in Mikah's bedchamber.

Mikah was standing on the opposite side of the room, dressed only in his loincloth. The Crimson Cloak lay on the bed.

"Mikah," Arenh said softly.

Mikah turned with a startled look and gazed at him in disbelief. "Arenh! How did you get here? You can't be here! You'll be caught and executed!"

"Please be calm, my friend," Arenh said. But secretly he was pleased that Mikah was concerned for his welfare. "I need to talk to you right away, but this isn't the place. I'll relocate us to my apartment if you'll trust me."

"Of course I trust you, Arenh. But we'll be lucky to escape with our lives if we're caught together!"

"All I need is for your body to be touching mine." Arenh realized too late that this didn't say very clearly what he had intended. In fact, it appeared to say something else altogether.

Mikah smiled in spite of his fear. "There hasn't been a day since we last touched that I haven't needed the same thing. But right now what we both need most is for you to leave quickly in whatever way you came!"

Arenh put his left hand on the Amulet and extended his right hand to Mikah. "Just come closer and take my hand."

Mikah didn't need to be invited a third time. The instant they touched they ceased to be in Mikah's chamber and were standing instead in Arenh's.

"We're in the Carnelian Cavern, in the heart of the Mountain," Arenh said. "We can talk safely."

"That's an incredible way to travel!" Mikah gasped. "I must be dreaming!"

"Maybe it is a dream," Arenh remarked, "but if it is, we're dreaming it together, which makes it indistinguishable from *reality* as far as I can tell."

Mikah thought, "I've heard rumors about teleportation devices, but I never believed them," not realizing that Arenh would know what he was thinking.

"The word *teleportation*," Arenh said with a pedantic tone, "implies we dematerialized in one place and materialized somewhere else. But nothing like that happens. It's just a matter of a larger than usual relocation. All motion is discontinuous. We move in jumps. Every particle of our bodies goes from here to there without passing through any point between. But ordinarily the relocations involved are so tiny that we perceive them as continuous movement."

"Thank you—I think," Mikah replied with amusement. "I didn't understand a word of that. But it doesn't matter. I'm so shocked you knew what I was thinking. I find that more upsetting than your powers of teleportation—or whatever it is you want to call it."

"I'm sorry about sensing your thoughts, Mikah. I'm not usually able to do it without the help of the Dreamers unless a person is close by. When someone is very near, it's hard not to do it, especially if I'm a bit anxious as I am now."

"You're forgiven," Mikah smiled. "Now tell me," he went on as he made a show of putting a little distance between himself and Arenh, "how far away do I need to stand for my thoughts to be private?"

"Actually, the Dreamers can know your thoughts anywhere and may choose to share them with me or not."

"My father told me of the Dreamers," Mikah said, as though he were talking more to himself than Arenh. "Very mysterious. He didn't understand what they were."

"Neither do I," Arenh admitted. "But I'm sure they're conscious entities like we are—just far more advanced in technology and far more evolved mentally. I doubt they have bodies anymore—not like ours, at least. My guess is they don't live in time and space at all, but they must have some way to localize their presence and influence. And that has something to do with what's in the peak of the Mountain, above the highest of the caverns that we know about."

"I'm still a bit upset that you can read my thoughts," Mikah said. "Friendship usually works better if the friends are on an equal footing. Don't you agree?"

"Yes, of course," Arenh agreed. "But I think the Dreamers may eventually burden you with similar abilities if you'll permit it to happen." Arenh hadn't thought about this before. But as he was saying it, he felt the accord of the Dreamers.

"Usually I insist on equal footing in any relationship," Mikah told him. "But I'll accept whatever footing I can get in your case."

"I love you too," Arenh said quietly. "I've thought of you every day since the last time I saw you. Losing my father and you on the same day was almost more than I could bear. At first I was so sad I couldn't stop crying. I even cried in my dreams." He felt his eyes moisten and fought back his emotions.

"You didn't lose me, my friend," Mikah said as he pulled Arenh into a hug and kissed him lightly on the lips.

In his younger years, Arenh had learned to cope with the dark passions of the soul—the loneliness and sadness and lack of hope—by losing himself in the passions of the body. But in the years since he had last seen Mikah, Arenh's sadness had become overwhelming.

Now, as he felt Mikah's lips on his, he felt those carnal passions stirring again that had lain dormant for so many years. The needs to escape his sadness and to make love to Mikah merged into an overpowering temptation. He pulled Mikah's body tight against his own and kissed him deeply. He

18

could feel that Mikah was becoming aroused. He let his hands slip down under Mikah's loincloth and grasped his buttocks lightly. "I'm happy to see," he whispered in Mikah's ear, "that you still have a nice firm butt."

"You should remember," Mikah whispered in reply, "that I am now the king."

"I'm sorry," Arenh pretended to apologize as he released Mikah and gently pushed him away, "what I meant to say was 'You still have a nice firm butt, *Your Majesty*'."

Mikah laughed. "I was just teasing, my friend. I didn't want you to stop, you know. I forgot how sensitive you are."

"It's been so long since I touched you, I think I got carried away." Arenh was a bit embarrassed.

"Well I hope you get carried away again soon!" Mikah laughed.

Arenh motioned for Mikah to sit beside him on the sofa. "There'll be more time later to renew our friendship," he assured Mikah. "But now, you and much of the City are in great danger. That's why I had to risk coming to see you.

"The valley people will soon launch another attack on the City walls. I believe this will be the second attack since you became king. In the first attack, you followed your father's custom of letting them cast the first stone from their catapult. Then after the stone bounced harmlessly off the City wall, you fired primitive projectile cannon to disable their machine, taking care to cause as few injuries as possible. Isn't that so?"

"Yes. But I wonder how you know this. Adhalmar does a good job of preventing any communication between the City and the Mountain. Did your lookouts observe the action and figure it out? Or did the Dreamers inform you?"

"Neither. Though it's true that the Dreamers usually tell me whatever I need to know—or to be more precise, whatever *they* need me to know—that didn't happen in this case. I know this sounds weird, but you told me about this yourself in a dream a few weeks ago."

"That's weird all right, even weirder than you think! I also recall a dream in which we talked about the attacks of the Ourdhu, and I explained why I used the projectile cannon."

"I had a hunch this might be happening," Arenh said. "We seem to have shared the same dream!"

"Let's keep this between me and you or they'll have us both in a psych ward," Mikah laughed.

"No doubt," Arenh agreed. "But I mentioned the projectile cannon because it's not a good idea to use it this time. This time the catapult will be throwing something the Ourdhu call a *demon's egg*, but which we would call a *low-yield antimatter bomb*."

Mikah was astonished. "Where would they get a weapon like that?"

"One of Adhalmar's agents gave it to them. He infiltrated the Ourdhu posing as a wizard. The device is physically quite small, so the Ourdhu have no idea it's a bomb. If they were to succeed in their plan to use it, it would detonate on impact and vaporize everything within a kilometer radius.

"Adhalmar chose to give them an antimatter weapon because it produces no radioactive contamination. The casualties would be enormous, but what's left of the City would still be inhabitable."

"I wonder what the Ourdhu expect to accomplish by this. Or even what Adhalmar expects to gain, for that matter."

"Adhalmar's agent has convinced the Ourdhu that when the demon's egg hatches, the demon will drive the City dwellers back into the Mountain. I think the war may have started when the Crimson and Emerald clans moved out of the Mountain over eight centuries ago. The valley people saw that as a threat.

"In any case, the demon's egg will wipe out a large part of the Crimson Sector, including the Palace and the barracks of the Guard. If you and the Royal Family survive, which isn't likely, the catastrophe will lead to a political crisis for you. Adhalmar will say that your compassion for our enemies is a weakness that disqualifies you for your position. You have no heir. So whether you survive the attack or not, he will accept the burden of becoming king."

"What do you think I should do?"

"The thoughts of the Dreamers are that you should foil Adhalmar's plan by departing from your expected modus operandi. The moment the catapult emerges from the eastern pass onto the high plain, you must use beam cannon to cut the ropes holding the throwing arm down. The flash of the beams will in itself frighten the Ourdhu.

"But more important, when the ropes are cut, the counterweight will drop. And the bomb will be hurled out into the plain. The blast will be frightening, but we should be able to avoid casualties on both sides. A welcome side effect will be that everyone in the City will embrace you as a hero, much to the disappointment of Lord Adhalmar."

"I haven't heard any intelligence reports about movement of the Ourdhu army," Mikah said. "Did the Dreamers say when this will happen?"

"They didn't say, but I'm sure it will be soon."

"Do they often foretell the future?"

"No. This is the first time."

Mikah appeared lost in thought for a few moments. Arenh stared at his friend's smooth, muscular physique and remembered their times together so many years before. He wanted to spend the night with Mikah, but he knew that wouldn't be wise.

"I share your desire," Mikah said in response to Arenh's thought, "but I agree it wouldn't be wise."

"Seems to me," Arenh smiled, "that my thoughts aren't so private anymore either."

Mikah had a momentary look of confusion and amazement on his face when he realized that Arenh had not said anything aloud.

"Our minds are becoming linked," Arenh told him. "The Dreamers have chosen you. Now that we have a way to get around Adhalmar's guards, I hope you will join me as often as you can in the zendo for mind training. Your mindlink with the Dreamers and with me will get even stronger if you do."

"I accept the invitation. Just remember, you're the chauffeur."

"Yes, and I can hardly wait to see you again, Mikah. But I better get you back to the Palace before you're missed, and for that I'll need your body in contact with mine again."

"My pleasure," Mikah said as they stood and embraced.

"Mine as well," Arenh smiled. Before the words were out of his mouth, they were back in Mikah's chamber, and someone was knocking at the door.

"Probably the chambermaid," Mikah whispered. He picked up his cloak from off the bed, and when he looked back to say goodbye, Arenh was gone. He fastened the Cloak around his shoulders and said, "You may enter."

Chapter 5—Mother

WHEN Arenh woke up the next morning, he heard the whispered thoughts of the Dreamers again. They told him that the Ourdhu had begun their march up the slopes towards the canyon that led to the high plain. They wouldn't emerge from the pass onto the plain until the next morning. Arenh also sensed Mikah's thoughts. The Dreamers had revealed the news of the Ourdhu march to him also.

Arenh had slept in the watchtower with the intention of getting up early enough to work for a while in the gardens. Working in the gardens helped to calm and clarify his mind. But the morning fog was already lifting when he woke up, and he had to be at the gymnasium soon after the guardsmen arrived. "Preparations for battle must begin right away," he thought. So he slung his cloak around his shoulders and left for the barracks.

He had just reached the upper entrance when he remembered his intention to tell his mother he had found the Amulet. In the emotional aftermath of seeing Mikah, he had forgotten. But he would pass the Amethyst Cavern on his way to the barracks, so he could stop and visit his mother for a few minutes.

He stopped a passing server bot and told it to send Lady Donna a message to expect him.

Meanwhile, when Mikah received the message from the Dreamers that the Ourdhu had begun their march, he summoned Jonah and briefed him on what was happening. He told Jonah to have his most trusted warriors prepare the beam cannon, but to do it secretly. He didn't want anyone else to know he was aware the Ourdhu were on the move.

"As soon as we get the official report that the Ourdhu are coming," Mikah told Jonah, "you should issue the usual orders to put the projectile cannon in place and load them. But if all goes as planned, of course, we won't need them."

By the time Mikah and Jonah had concluded their meeting, Arenh was entering the foyer that led to the quarters of Lady Julia.

"Your mother is expecting you," Donna said. She seemed amused. Donna often seemed amused. "She's been a little upset that she hasn't seen you much of late," Donna continued, clearly pleased at the anxiety her remark created in Arenh.

"Yes. I've been preoccupied."

"A young lady perhaps?" Donna teased with a raised eyebrow.

"You wish," Arenh smiled. He liked Donna and trusted her completely. She had been his mother's lady-in-waiting for as long as he could remember. "I've seen Mikah again." He said it as though it weren't important.

"Oh my!" Donna seemed shocked. "That was most dangerous!" she whispered. "I don't think I should hear any more about it right now. Perhaps later, in a more private place. I don't think it would be wise to speak to your mother about this. Do you?"

"I think I'll need to talk to her about it sooner or later," Arenh whispered back. "And I would prefer later, of course."

Donna smiled. "She's waiting for you," she said softly.

Arenh had been standing with his left side towards Donna. But as he turned to walk away, she could see his fully exposed body on his right side, where his chlamys was open.

"Arenh!" she called out sharply. He stopped and looked at her. "You don't appear to be wearing a tunic under your cloak."

"Yes, I seem to have forgotten it again," he said sheepishly. "I'll take care to keep my left side towards my mother."

"Wait, I have a clasp," Donna offered. "We'll fasten the chlamys under your right arm to keep it closed." She worked a few moments with the clasp. "There, that should help," she said after the deed was done. "There are some things a mother shouldn't have to see." A coy grin and a quick glance down let him know that she herself, however, didn't mind seeing such things at all.

Lady Julia had two cups of tea poured when Arenh entered her parlor. She was seated at a small but elegant table. The room was spacious, sparsely furnished, and beautifully lit by several false windows, which glowed with a soft even light.

Arenh admired her dress, a floor-length pale blue chiton with a belt woven from cords of gold and indigo. Her earrings of pale blue sapphires matched her necklace of the same stones. He noticed the clasp holding her hair up was also covered with sapphires. She had a little apricot poodle at her feet.

Arenh worried about her. He worried about everybody, of course. But he worried especially about his mother. After his father's death, she had withdrawn to her apartment and seldom came out. Arenh had asked her to join him in presiding over official occasions and ceremonies, much as she had with his father. But she had refused.

His mother was beautiful he thought. Not just for a woman of her age, but for a woman of any age. She was one of the first to undergo regeneration, shortly after the bio-regenerators had been discovered. The machines appeared to use a person's own stem cells and a time dilation device to rebuild tissue in a very short time span. They could heal wounds and cure diseases, and some people thought they could even restore life to the dead. Arenh doubted that. But his mother was beautiful proof that they could reverse the damage of the aging process.

"Come," she said. "Our tea will be cold." His mother had a way of commanding others that made them *want* to obey.

"Good morning." Arenh leaned over to kiss her forehead. "I'm sorry I can't stay for long this morning, but I have some good news or what I hope is good news."

"There hasn't been much of that lately. Please sit down and tell me."

"I found the Amulet," he said as he sat down.

"Wonderful! Do you have it on?"

"Yes." Arenh carefully removed the chain and Amulet from his neck with one hand while holding his cloak in place with the other. He handed the artifact to his mother, who looked at it carefully.

Meanwhile, her poodle began to hump Arenh's leg. "We haven't been properly introduced," Arenh protested in a whisper. But the little creature continued with even more energy than before.

"Yes. That's it," his mother said in a low voice while gazing intently at the Amulet. Then she said more strongly, "You must never take it off again. Do you think you can discover how to—" She suddenly noticed her poodle's infatuation with Arenh. "Achilles!" she commanded sharply, "Stop that this instant!"

Achilles stopped and jumped up in Arenh's lap and began to lick him in the mouth.

"As I was saying, do you think you can discover how to use it?"

"I've used it already," Arenh said—between attempts to dodge Achilles' tongue. He regretted what he had said immediately. "How stupid," he thought.

"I see," his mother said as she handed the Amulet to Arenh and took Achilles in her arms. "Well I don't need two guesses to know what you used it for," she continued as Arenh put the Amulet around his neck again. "How is His Majesty?"

"He's well at the moment. But I fear for him. The Dreamers sent me to warn him of a danger they've foreseen in the near future."

"One doesn't need to foresee the future to know it's filled with danger for Mikah," she said as she

28

lifted her cup for a sip of tea. "You can spare me the details."

"Thank you. It's best not to speak of it any more than necessary."

"You say the Dreamers sent you to him?" she asked and then continued as usual without waiting for an answer, "Did the Dreamers also lead you to the Amulet?"

"Yes and not exactly," he replied. "I did say the Dreamers sent me to warn Mikah. And though I said I found the Amulet, it would be more accurate to say it found me. The Dreamers materialized it on the altar while I was sitting in the zendo. They listen now while we talk. Or maybe that's a simplification of reality necessary for those of us who are confined to space and time. They already know what we're going to say. Or perhaps from their point of view, we have already said it. Or maybe we are always and forever saying it."

"They foresee the future," his mother declared, as though that explained everything in her mind. "Your father told me on several occasions that to foresee the future is to change the future. For that reason, he told me, we must refrain from efforts to see into the future."

"Father was a wise man. I miss him very much. And I think he was right. Of course, we all have to consider what various turns the flow of events may take in the future so we can be prepared. But those are merely expectations or guesses or hunches. The Dreamers don't guess."

"You believe then that the Dreamers determine the future?"

He saw the importance of the question. If the Dreamers determined the future, then they had sent her husband to his death. And would they do the same to her son after they had used him for their purposes?

"No," he told her. "In the world of the Dreamers, I believe there's no future for them to determine. I believe it's we ourselves who direct the course of history. We puny little creatures of time and space determine the future by our choices." He realized from his mother's facial expression that his voice had grown bitter.

She put her hand on his and said in a comforting voice, "Your tea is getting cold, my dear."

He leaned over and hugged her. "I have to go now. I'll visit again as soon as I can, and I promise that next time I'll stay long enough to finish my tea. I love you."

"I love you too. Take care, my son. And Arenh," she switched back to her commanding voice, "when you visit next time—wear your tunic!"

He felt his face blush and mumbled, "Yes ma'am."

Chapter 6—The plan

ARENH went from his mother's apartment to the Jasper Cavern, which contained the barracks and gymnasium of the Indigo Guard. Ordinarily he made semi-annual visits to inspect the Guard. And while they were officially unscheduled, everyone knew within a day or two of when they would occur. This would be his first truly unexpected visit, but Arenh knew he would be welcome.

Arenh had been pleased with the way Kodhi had integrated the androids with the human guards. Kodhi felt at ease with the androids, and his rapport with the human warriors enabled him to ease their anxieties about working with the robots.

As Arenh entered, Kodhi saw him. "A-ten-HUT!" he shouted. The men and women in the gym quickly obeyed, coming to attention wherever they were. Kodhi walked to where Arenh was standing. "My Lord!" he exclaimed with a slight bow. "We're honored by your visit!"

Arenh looked around the room full of warriors. They were all completely naked. And except for his helmet, which partially covered the neural implants in his skull, so was Kodhi. The pretenses of rank and aristocracy were difficult to maintain when everyone was naked. It helped in the process of rooting authority in knowledge and competence. Arenh knew, nevertheless, that Kodhi's troops would have been in full battle dress if they had known he was coming.

"Please put your troops at ease, Captain," Arenh told Kodhi.

"As you were!" Kodhi shouted. The warriors in the room quickly scurried towards the hooks on the gym wall where their gear was hanging. Soon Kodhi was the only person in the room who was completely undressed.

"Let's find a private place to talk a moment," Arenh said.

Kodhi took his chlamys from a hook on a nearby wall and swung it over his shoulder. "Certainly, this way, sir."

When they were settled in Kodhi's office, Arenh told him of the expected attack from the Ourdhu and of the treachery he and Mikah suspected.

"The Ourdhu won't be the problem," Arenh said. "The problem will be the Emerald Lord. When Mikah foils Adhalmar's plans, we should be prepared for war."

"I've been praying for this day," Kodhi replied. "The thing that upsets me most about Adhalmar is that we can kill him only once."

"I would like to think, Kodhi, that I'm free from such revengeful motives. But the truth is, I often feel as you do. In any case, our primary objectives are to prevent loss of life as much as possible and to protect the king."

"And to empower him to restore the Council?"

"Yes. I think that would be certain to happen if we defeat the Emerald forces."

"What's your plan?"

"You and I will meet with Mikah and his captain, Jonah, to finalize our plans. Meanwhile, I need for you to select a hundred of our best warriors and our most capable commander to lead them. Each of the warriors will in turn command a squad which can include androids as well as human guardsmen."

"Our most capable warriors, My Lord, are often androids," Kodhi said with a smile. "I agree though that all those in the line of command must be human. And at the risk of seeming immodest, I must say that I am myself our most capable commander."

"I'll depend entirely on your judgment," Arenh told him.

"It will be as you command, My Lord."

Arenh provided a verbal list of the numbers of androids, robotic troop carriers, and warbots he thought would be needed to support the human guardsmen. Kodhi respectfully suggested different numbers.

"Again, I will depend entirely on your judgment," Arenh replied.

As Arenh walked back to his apartment, he sensed the thoughts and emotions of Mikah. "And what *is* our plan?" Mikah whispered in Arenh's mind. Mikah's parroting of some of Kodhi's words led Arenh to believe the Dreamers had made him a party to at least some of Arenh's conversation with Kodhi.

"Maybe I could meet you in your chamber to talk," Arenh thought to Mikah.

"I'm there now," was Mikah's response.

Arenh relocated to Mikah's apartment and found Mikah waiting this time. He was at a small table with tea ready. Arenh sat down and began to share with him a plan to have a hundred squads of the most capable Indigo warriors ready to enter battle on a moment's notice.

"I assume your troops will be transported by the equipment you requisitioned from Kodhi," Mikah said. "But I'm not familiar with your war machines, and I don't know how you would get them into battle."

"We have fast fighter planes we call *warbots* and armored aerial troop carriers. They're both launched from hangars built into the high cliffs on the west side of the Mountain, overlooking the Western Sea. They can't be seen from the City as they're launched. The carriers are like tanks when they land. We have androids who serve alongside our human guardsmen, and the warbots and carriers are equipped with the same artificial intelligence module as the androids. They all need only a minimum of direction from our commanders, which is supplied by direct neural links based on quantum entanglement."

"Merciful Mother!" Mikah exclaimed. "Why are we sneaking around? If I had at my disposal what you have, Adhalmar would be a footnote in someone's history book by now!"

"What's at my disposal is also at your disposal," Arenh said. "But I think the adage that *power corrupts*

34

is true. I just hope we don't *become* the very evil we're trying to *overcome*."

"If things keep going as they have for the past ten years, I think we may need to worry more about staying alive long enough to become anything."

"That's what we're trying to do, isn't it?"

"Right. Of course. I'll direct Jonah to select three hundred of the best in the Crimson Guard. Our Guard isn't large enough for a hundred squads. We'll be prepared to transport them all by armored airborne carriers. We'll need a few men to manage the beam cannon. We'll also have a team to man the projectile cannon, so we don't arouse Adhalmar's suspicions. I'll ask Jonah to coordinate with Kodhi as soon as you can make him available. They can work out command details between them."

"I wonder ..." Arenh hesitated.

"If we can trust Jonah," Mikah finished his sentence for him.

Arenh nodded.

"I trust him completely. He's married to my sister. And my wife, Leah, is his sister. But even if there were no family bonds, I would trust him."

Arenh felt Mikah's affection for Leah when he said her name. He had known Mikah was married. As the Indigo Lord, Arenh could adopt an heir if he had no blood relative to succeed him, but marriage and children were required by law for the Crimson Lord. Such marriages were often more political than personal. Sometimes, however, a political union developed over time into an intimate personal relationship as well. Now he wondered about the nature of the relationship between Mikah and Leah.

He felt something he hadn't felt before. Was it jealousy?

"Yes, of course, it's jealousy," Mikah said in a soft voice without the least hint of condemnation.

"I'm sorry I feel that way," Arenh said. "Jealousy has nothing to do with real love."

"You never cut yourself any slack, do you Arenh?"

"You think feeling regret is bad?"

"No. It's just that jealousy is such a common feeling for me," Mikah explained. "I don't feel any regret, though, for feeling jealous. I do see how destructive it can be. It's just that jealousy is enough of a challenge without having to deal with regret too.

"Anyway, you have no reason to be jealous of Leah. She's a loyal friend, and I confide in her often. But our marriage is one of convenience.

"Sometimes I wish she would show some sexual interest in me. We need to have a baby—we have to produce an heir. But I find it hard to be interested in someone who doesn't seem interested in me, and she devotes most of her attention to her lover, a young nobleman."

Arenh could feel pain from Mikah as he mentioned Leah's lover.

"He's one of a series," Mikah continued. "I don't even know his name. He's also in a marriage of convenience. I think he's mainly a sexual toy for her. In any case, I'm certain she doesn't confide in him the way she does in me.

"She knew of my predilection for other males before we were married," Mikah said, "so my

36

relationship with you is no betrayal of her. She's happy that you and I can see each other again. I want you to meet her—soon. But right now, time is growing short. We need to put a wrap on our plans. When will your troops and their transports be ready?"

"I'll ask Kodhi to have them ready today by the 19th hour. Do you think we need to ask Jonah and Kodhi to join us for a strategy meeting just to be sure we're all on the same page? Or at least in the same book?"

"I can have Jonah here in a few minutes, but how will you get Kodhi here?"

"The same way I relocated the two of us earlier."

"All right. But I don't want you to hold him the way you held me. Okay?"

"Wow! I see what you meant by saying that jealousy is a common feeling for you," Arenh laughed. "You're so straightforward about it. And while I admit I'm glad you're a little jealous, more than a little wouldn't be good for either of us. Anyway, I'll only need to touch Kodhi's hand. I'll go and get him now."

They embraced. Then Arenh stepped away from Mikah. He breathed out as he put his hand over the Amulet. And when he breathed in, he was in the Jasper Cavern within the Mountain. He went to the gym to find Kodhi, but learned he had gone home already. So he went to Kodhi's apartment and knocked.

Kodhi called out for him to enter, not knowing who it was. When he saw Arenh, he tried to get up from his chair, but Arenh stopped him. Kodhi was seated with his wife standing behind him. She was applying some kind of solution to the implants in his skull.

"This is my wife, Erika. I'm sorry you have to see us like this, My Lord. But the contacts for the implants must be cleaned before we enter battle. It's a chore Erika does well."

"I think we're done for the time being," Erika said. "We're honored by your visit, My Lord. I'll leave you two alone to discuss your plans."

Kodhi motioned for Arenh to sit down. Arenh suddenly realized he was staring at Kodhi. Kodhi noticed too.

"My apologies for staring," Arenh said. "This is the first time I've seen you without your helmet on." Kodhi's head was clean-shaven, and on each side of his head, just above his ears, was a metallic object that looked like a small horn protruding from the skin.

"I keep my whole head shaved," Kodhi explained, "because it doesn't look as weird as having little round bald spots where the implants are."

"I just now realize how many sacrifices some of you make to assure the safety of the rest of us," Arenh said.

"I may look like a freak," Kodhi answered, a little embarrassed. "But it's not really much of a sacrifice. The implants are like a part of me now. I receive info through them all the time. But when I'm connected directly in two-way communication with the androids, I'm like a different person. The machines have no emotions, and I begin to lose mine. I like it in some ways—maybe too much.

"At first I always held on to fear. I thought fear was the thing that made me human—fear of dying, fear of losing loved ones, fear of losing my soul. I thought fear brought me back to Erika and to the rest of the human race."

"That surprises me," Arenh replied. "I've always thought of fear as an enemy."

"I eventually came to see that," Kodhi said. "Fear will paralyze you when you need to move and then leave you when you need it to keep you from doing something reckless. I've come to see that love is the only thing you can depend on. Love always brings me back. The machines don't know about it. I respect the machines. I guess I admire them because they have no fear. But I have to keep reminding myself. They have no love either. But I'm sure you didn't come here to discuss my feelings about love."

"We're the two leaders of our clan, Kodhi. It's important for us to know each other well. And that means we need to share our feelings about the things that matter most.

"I remember when you met me at the lower entrance right after my father was murdered. Jonah had told me only a few hours before that your father had taken his own life when he learned of the assassination. It was so senseless. And yet, though we both lost our fathers at about the same time and both their deaths were tragic and senseless, you and I have never talked about it."

"Some things are so painful it's hard to talk about them. At first I was afraid you blamed my father for your father's death. I knew that wasn't true when you appointed me to take my father's place. I think you have no idea what that meant to me."

"Your father blamed himself for something he was powerless to prevent."

"Yes. I wish I had realized that and talked to him in time," Kodhi said.

"You and I were both too young then to know what to do," Arenh told him. "But I'm confident we'll do better in dealing with the crisis facing us now. We'll right some wrongs, my friend. We owe it to our fathers.

"I don't want to rush you, but when you can get to it, I need a report on your progress in getting the troops and equipment together that we talked about."

"Not a problem," Kodhi said. "I have the entire battle group assembled as you ordered. They're camped in the hangars of the transport vehicles. We're ready to go on a moment's notice."

"Very good," Arenh said. "I hope you have time now to go with me to Mikah's palace for a strategy session with him and Jonah."

Kodhi appeared a little confused. "How do we get there?" he asked. "Without showing our hand, I mean?"

"Let's get your helmet back on first," Arenh said. "Do you need Erika for that?"

"Oh no," Kodhi replied as he reached for his helmet and positioned it on his head.

"Best to stand up, then take my hand and breathe out," Arenh instructed him.

Kodhi looked a little puzzled as he stood and cautiously took Arenh's hand. Then he gasped for breath as he found himself in the Crimson Palace with Mikah and Jonah staring at him.

"Your Majesty!" Kodhi said as he bowed to Mikah.

"Formalities won't be necessary here, Kodhi," Mikah smiled. "Say hello to Jonah. The two of you will be directing this operation together."

Kodhi was still a little stunned, but managed to nod to Jonah.

"I'm sorry, Kodhi," Arenh said. "I should have told you what to expect."

Jonah, who also appeared a little shocked, said to Mikah, "A little information about what to expect on this end would have been helpful too."

"Now Jonah," Mikah chided, "a soldier should always be ready for the unexpected."

"Yeah," Jonah agreed. "But we usually expect the unexpected from our enemies, not our friends."

"One of our sociologists did a study," Arenh commented, "in which she discovered that most violent disturbances of the peace occur on weekends and holidays among family and friends. Her conclusion was that we should beware of family and friends on weekends and holidays."

They all laughed. "Good thing," Mikah added, "that today isn't a weekend or a holiday!" Arenh could see that Jonah and Kodhi enjoyed the implication that they were friends and family.

41

When their strategy session was over and Jonah had left, Arenh took Kodhi back to the Mountain. Then later in the day, after the evening meal, Arenh returned to Mikah.

"I have to confess," Mikah told him with a lustful look, "that I could hardly take my eyes off Kodhi."

"I'm sure he noticed. You looked like a dog with his tongue hanging out."

"I wasn't that obvious!" Mikah protested. "Besides, looking does no harm, does it?"

"Of course not," Arenh agreed. "But Kodhi is a lover of women. He's married to a beautiful woman, and he's totally devoted to her. The obvious attentions of another man may make him a little uncomfortable."

"So you just pretend that Adonis isn't standing there?"

"Yes. I believe that pretense is the lubrication for the wheels of society."

"Well, I'll try to be less transparent. But Kodhi is hot! And I'm only human."

"If lust is what makes us human, my mother's little poodle is more human than all of us," Arenh laughed.

"Great Mother!" Mikah exclaimed. "Now the man's calling me a horny poodle!"

"Not really," Arenh laughed. "But any time you *feel* like a horny poodle, you can hump *my* leg— unless, of course, we're preoccupied with something like dodging the blasts from Adhalmar's beam weapons."

"That's a promise?" Mikah grinned.

"That's a promise. But the Ourdhu will be reaching the high plain by early morning, and I need to get some sleep right now."

"Can you stay the night?" Mikah asked.

"I was hoping you would ask. I like being close to you. But as I said, I need to get some sleep."

"But I'm having that horny poodle feeling again," Mikah confided. "And you said I could hump your leg. You promised."

"Tell you what, then," Arenh conceded, "why don't you have fun with one of my legs while I roll over and get some sleep?"

"My choice?"

"Your choice."

Chapter 7—The battle

ARENH woke up the next morning several hours before daylight. Mikah was lying on his side with an arm across Arenh's chest. Arenh tried to extract himself from his friend's embrace without waking him, but failed.

"Good morning, My Lord Arenh," Mikah yawned. "You have a nice leg."

"Good morning, Your Majesty. I'm happy you enjoyed it."

"I'd like to enjoy it some more. I wish you didn't have to go."

"Me too, but I can't keep Kodhi waiting." A mischievous grin came on Arenh's face as he fastened his tunic.

"Everybody thinks you're so nice, Arenh," Mikah said sleepily. "But you have a mean little streak they don't know about."

"Yeah. It's our little secret," Arenh smiled. He bent over and kissed Mikah on the forehead as he touched the Amulet.

Mikah started to answer, but Arenh was no longer there.

After Arenh had relocated to the Mountain, Mikah got up, dressed, and walked to the barracks to meet Jonah. Jonah informed him they had received the report shortly after midnight that the Ourdhu were entering the canyon that led to the high plain.

"They won't reach the narrow pass that opens to the plain until just before dawn," Jonah observed. "Their commander is wise. He plans to emerge from the pass with the rising sun behind him."

Jonah updated Mikah as to the status of their forces. He had issued an order to deploy the projectile cannon in a noisy and noticeable way while secretly arming the large beam cannon that were installed in a tower on the city wall. He had ordered these weapons pointed towards the place where the eastern pass opened into the plain.

Mikah was pleased. He sent his thoughts to Arenh and felt Arenh's acknowledgment in return.

Shortly after sunrise, the catapult began to emerge from the pass. The Ourdhu used it as a shield for their infantry. Jonah immediately ordered the beam cannon to be aimed. As soon as the gunners indicated the weapons were locked on their targets, he gave the order to fire. The words were scarcely out of his mouth when the brilliant streaks of energy tore through the air followed quickly by rolling claps of thunder.

The ropes holding down the throwing arm of the catapult vaporized at the points of their attachment. And though Jonah had set the weapons to their lowest energy levels, parts of the catapult blew apart. The arm swiftly lurched forward, then stopped abruptly as the falling counterweight caught on one of the broken beams of the machine.

The bomb was hurled upward on a trajectory that landed it far too close to the catapult.

The blindingly bright flash came first. It made no sound whatever. It grew in intensity for a second or two and then faded. A few more seconds of eerie silence came next during which an ugly mushroom of darkness and fire—which was also beautiful in a way—raised itself into the air. Then came a loud, sharp CRACK like a projectile cannon blast followed by a rumbling, growling roar that continued on and on like an approaching tornado.

The blast wave rolled eastward towards the pass—knocking down everything in its path, including the fleeing Ourdhu—and westward to hit the wall of the City like the combination of a major tremor and a hurricane.

Mikah whispered, "My God, Jonah! What have we done?"

Jonah had taken the precaution of having all available medical corpsmen standing by. He ordered them into troop carriers and sent them speeding at low altitude across the plain towards the pass. Mikah and Jonah with their personal guards followed the medics in an armored aircar. The remaining troops of the Crimson Clan followed in armored airborne carriers.

At the same time in the Mountain, Arenh sensed the thoughts of the Dreamers: the image of an emerald serpent striking and the word *now* pronounced with a hissing sound.

"Adhalmar will strike now," Arenh told Kodhi. "Let's do it."

Kodhi stared blankly, and his affect flattened as he merged his mind into the neural network of the robotics and silently gave the GO command. The carriers loaded with guardsmen and androids began to pour from their hangar bays on the western cliff like bats from their caves. The warbots were hurled at full speed from their launch tubes below the hangars with a steady pop-pop-pop-pop that sounded like heavy artillery fire.

Arenh put his left hand over the Amulet and his right hand on Kodhi's shoulder, and the two of them found themselves near what was left of the Ourdhu catapult.

Jonah spotted Arenh and Kodhi and ordered their car towards that location. He directed the Crimson fleet to follow. The Indigo carriers had just arrived and their troops were disembarking when Mikah's aircar landed.

Mikah and Jonah had hardly emerged from their ship when Arenh pointed towards the City. A huge fleet of troop carriers followed by fighter planes was speeding from the Emerald Sector towards the pass. As the Emerald carriers sat down on the plain, the fighters swept over them and opened fire without warning. The obvious aim of the Emerald attack was to eliminate Mikah and Arenh and their captains at all costs. This at least spared most of the remaining Crimson and Indigo forces for the moment.

At the instant the Emerald ships opened fire, the first wave of Indigo warbots appeared as if from nowhere and dropped like falcons into the Emerald formation from above. The quantum targeting computers of the warbots were a thousand times faster than their Emerald counterparts, which were too slow to get a lock on their fast-moving Indigo targets. And the quantum communication among the Indigo machines was instantaneous, which prevented any duplication in targeting. The warbots downed the entire force of enemy fighters within a few minutes. Then they turned their guns on the Emerald troop carriers, blowing most of them apart while they were still on the ground.

The Emerald fleet was in ruins. Adhalmar's surviving troop carriers, presumably with him aboard, turned tail and fled back towards the City with the warbots in pursuit. All eyes were turned towards the chase as the warbots knocked down one after another of the fleeing carriers.

"Break it off, Kodhi!" Arenh ordered.

"As you command, My Lord," Kodhi replied.

Arenh noticed a coldness in Kodhi's voice that he had never heard before. And he felt a silent darkness, a terrible loneliness he couldn't explain. He turned his head towards Kodhi. He glimpsed for an instant the sensor rods that had dropped from Kodhi's helmet and that were pressed against the implants in his skull. And then Arenh's eye caught something else beyond Kodhi—lying on the ground. Mikah had been hit!

"Miikaah!" Arenh shouted as he ran towards his friend's body lying on the blackened and flattened grass of the plain. But Mikah didn't answer. His head was perfectly intact, but his eyes were fixed in the stare of death. His chest was torn open, and part of a broken rib was exposed. And deep within the charred and bloody hole where the left pectoral muscle used to be, Arenh could see that only part of the heart and left lung remained.

"I will destroy them all!" The thought blazed across Arenh's mind like wildfire. But then his mind went clear and cold as ice as he scooped Mikah's corpse into his arms.

"Kodhi! Transport our wounded and the Ourdhu to the Mountain. Jonah! Collect the Emerald and follow Kodhi!"

Arenh didn't wait for them to signal compliance. He pulled Mikah's limp body against the Amulet and found himself standing in front of one of the bio-regenerators deep within the Mountain.

"Lay him here," a voice said.

Chapter 8—The aftermath

ARENH laid Mikah's body on a platform in front of the regenerator, stripped off the bloody cloak and loincloth, and then realized that Wahlis, the chief medic, was the voice that had spoken. Wahlis pushed the button that slid the platform into the machine. The regenerator looked like a large metallic tube about three meters in length. The circular door closed automatically when the platform was inside.

"I don't think there was much left to his heart and left lung," Arenh said. "Is there any hope?" His voice cracked.

"Don't despair." Dr. Wahlis spoke softly and slowly. "We've never tried regeneration with injuries this extensive, but the machine may be able to rebuild the destroyed organs and tissues and restore life provided the brain cells were not destroyed."

"His head appeared to be untouched," Arenh said, grasping for even the slightest hope.

"Yes," Wahlis reassured him. "I believe the brain is structurally intact. The issue will be the length of the interval in which the cells were deprived of blood."

"How long does the regeneration process take?"

"Only a few minutes usually. But with damage this extensive, I don't really know."

Arenh waited in front of the regenerator for over an hour. The minutes passed slowly as he paced back and forth. He refused the offers of the medical staff to wait in a more comfortable place or even to sit in a chair within sight of the machine. Occasionally he glanced anxiously at the circular door. And just when his last glimmer of hope began to fade, the door of the cylinder opened to reveal Mikah's feet on the platform.

There was silence for a moment. Then a voice came from inside, "Am I in heaven or is this the other place?"

"It was the other place before we heard your voice," Arenh laughed through his tears, "but it's heaven now!"

"I'm dead!?" Mikah asked in alarm.

"You were dead," Wahlis told him calmly as he pushed the button that extracted the platform, "but you're very much alive now, Your Majesty." The medic picked up a small blanket and covered Mikah with it.

"Let's get you up as quickly as we can," Arenh said. "We have many more wounded waiting."

"What happened?" Mikah asked.

"Let's leave Dr. Wahlis and his staff to their work, and I'll tell you as we walk. Thank you, Doctor!"

"Thank *you*, My Lord," the medic replied.

Arenh wrapped the blanket around Mikah and tied it like a loincloth. "He's more beautiful than ever," he thought.

51

"You think the nicest things," Mikah said. And Arenh realized the dark loneliness he had felt on the battlefield was gone.

Arenh held the remains of the Crimson Cloak in one arm and wrapped his other arm around Mikah's bare shoulders, holding his own cloak so that it draped over both their backs. They walked slowly towards Arenh's apartment while Arenh breathed out gratitude for the warmth of Mikah's skin against his own.

They paused a moment as medical corpsmen rushed past them with a wounded Emerald guardsman on a stretcher that seemed to float in the air like a boat in water. They could see similar airborne stretchers with wounded soldiers on them hovering in one of the side corridors. Server bots floated among them administering fluids and medications under the direction of androids, which had been reprogrammed as nurses for triage and first-phase treatment.

As they walked on, Mikah said in a sad voice, "You were wondering back there how many may have died waiting for a machine while those of us who were more fortunate were in the regenerators."

"Yes," Arenh replied, "and unfortunately I wasn't able to hide those thoughts from you."

"You don't need to hide anything from me, my love."

They arrived at Arenh's apartment. After they entered and Mikah was resting comfortably on a sofa, Arenh asked, "What's the last thing you remember on the battlefield?"

"I remember you pointing towards the City."

"I was pointing at the Emerald fleet." Arenh then recounted what happened after that up to the point when Mikah awoke in the hospital. He had just finished the update when Jonah and Kodhi entered.

"We'll have to change your name to Lazarus," Jonah said as he leaned over and kissed Mikah on the forehead.

Leah had meanwhile entered the room behind Jonah. "They told me you were dead!" she sobbed when she saw Mikah. Mikah stood up and hugged her silently for a few moments.

"He's okay now, Sis," Jonah said comfortingly.

Leah pulled herself together. "What a frightening day!" she said as Mikah sat down again and motioned for her to sit beside him.

"Thank you, Mikah." She sat down and began to tell them of the damage she had seen in the Palace. "There's hardly a window left intact. Dishes broken. Glass everywhere. Furniture toppled, sometimes on top of people. So many hurt!"

Meanwhile, Arenh signaled one of the server bots and gave it an order for drinks and food. And when Leah had finished her report of conditions in the Palace, he said, "I ordered for you too, Leah. None of us has had much opportunity to eat or rest."

"Thank you, Arenh. But the best thing for me is to return to the Palace. Our entire household is in turmoil. And I know this isn't nearly over. You have a lot to discuss."

"I'll walk you to your car," Arenh volunteered. As they walked to the hangar bay where Leah's aircar was parked, he could sense her thoughts.

"I see why Mikah is so much in love with him," she was thinking. "I wish he cared as much for me."

"You're very much in love with Mikah," he told her. "I feel it."

"Yes. I've been trying for years to get his attention. I've even brought young men into my chamber right in front of him and made love to them loudly, but I haven't aroused even a spark of jealousy in him!" Her voice sounded weary.

"He loves you too, Leah—very deeply," Arenh assured her. "But he may take your affairs with other men to mean a lack of interest in *him*. I think Mikah isn't able to be sexual with someone if he feels that person isn't attracted to him. That's just the way he is."

"If what you say is true," Leah replied pensively, "we've somehow fallen into a terrible state of misunderstanding. In reality, I'm more attracted to him than to anyone I've ever met!"

When they arrived at her car, Leah tiptoed slightly and kissed Arenh on the lips. "You're just as sweet as he told me you were," she said.

When Arenh returned to his apartment, the other men were already sitting at the table eating. Arenh sat down in front of his tray.

"Jonah wanted to eat your share of the food," Kodhi lied. "But I wouldn't let him."

"The truth is," Jonah laughed, "he ate his share, then the plate you ordered for Leah, and then he was reaching for your tray when Mikah stopped him."

"Thanks, Mikah," Arenh smiled. "But I'm not really hungry." He shoved his tray towards Kodhi, who nodded his thanks and continued eating as if he were starving. "He probably hasn't taken time to eat in the last two days," Arenh thought.

Meanwhile, Kodhi didn't let eating get in the way of business. "Where do we go from here?" he asked, hardly taking time to swallow first.

"I suggest," Arenh answered, "that we start with three royal decrees: First, restore the Council; second, restore the Indigo Lord to the office of prime minister; and third, arrest Adhalmar and charge him with murder and high treason."

"Couldn't have said it better myself," Kodhi said.

"Consider it done, Mr. Prime Minister," Mikah agreed. "I'll have the documents issued as soon as you get me back to the Palace."

Jonah, always the cautious one, warned that arresting Adhalmar wouldn't be easy. "Adhalmar will fight."

Kodhi nodded his head in agreement, and then looked Arenh straight in the eye with a startled look.

"Arenh! I just received a communication from the androids!" he said excitedly. "They believe they've identified one of the Emerald troops who just went through regeneration as Prince Karl, the son of Adhalmar!"

They all looked at each other in astonishment. Then Arenh said quietly, "I suggest, Kodhi, that you and Jonah go right away to detain our noble guest safely. And treat him with respect and dignity."

After the two captains had left to take the Emerald prince into custody, Mikah seemed pleased. "An idea just occurred to me," he said. But when he looked at Arenh, he knew that he had no need to say what it was.

"I think that's a devious idea," Arenh said accusingly.

"Yes, my love. That's why *you* didn't think of it. Would you tell Jonah and Kodhi to bring Karl to me?"

After the captains had returned with Prince Karl, Arenh told them they could wait outside the room. Kodhi objected, but Arenh assured him that Karl was no threat to the two of them.

Kodhi briefly glanced at the slightly-built Emerald Prince from head to toe. "Yes, I suppose not," he agreed.

"You think I'm no threat because I'm not as big as His Majesty or Lord Arenh?" Karl asked Kodhi.

Kodhi was startled. Arenh smiled.

"No offense intended, Your Highness," Kodhi apologized. And to Arenh, he said, "We'll wait right outside the door, and I'll leave one of the androids inside if that meets with your approval, My Lord."

Arenh nodded his consent.

After Mikah and Arenh had talked to Karl, they summoned Jonah and Kodhi and asked them to accompany the Prince back to his quarters.

"What did you think of him?" Mikah asked after the captains had taken Karl away.

"I was impressed at how gentle he is."

"Me too," Mikah agreed. "I feel guilty using him as we are, but it's necessary."

"I think he understands what's going on," Arenh assured him, "and he's okay with it. I sensed Karl's thoughts and probed his memories. I may owe my life to him. His father had intended to have me assassinated before I could assume the Cloak. Jonah had suspected that as I recall. But Karl convinced his father that wouldn't be wise. The son appears to have more wisdom than the father."

"Or at least more compassion," Mikah said.

"I don't think one is possible without the other."

"I think you're right," Mikah agreed. "His mother is another story though."

"Yes. I've never met Lady Katrina. But I've heard that people in the Emerald Clan fear her as much as they do Adhalmar. If so, that's certain to bring her into conflict with her own son."

Chapter 9—Justice

THE NEXT morning, Arenh ordered Kodhi to take Karl and a couple of androids by aircar to the lower entrance. Their tasks in order of importance were to unlock the entrance and open the door, take the two Emerald guardsmen assigned there into custody, and then reassign the guards to accompany Prince Karl to the Emerald Palace. The logical sequence of the tasks, however, required the guards to be taken into custody first.

When the aircar landed in front of the entrance, the Emerald guards bravely pointed their weapons at the Indigo shield on its door. But when the door opened and Prince Karl appeared, they lowered their weapons and came to attention. Then when Kodhi and the androids emerged with weapons drawn, the guards were totally confused.

"Surrender your weapons to Captain Kodhi," Karl ordered. One of the guards complied immediately. The other hesitated.

"I will be *Lord* Karl before the end of the day, soldier!" Karl snapped harshly.

The guardsman surrendered his weapon and dropped to his knees in front of Karl.

"No need to grovel," Karl told him softly. "But never question my orders again."

Kodhi glanced at Karl with a look of obvious admiration. He then directed one of the androids to remove the bolt that locked the door. Karl and the two guardsmen flinched as the robot held the door with one hand, then grasped the bolt with the other and ripped it from its mountings with no apparent effort.

Kodhi opened the door to the lower entrance.

Karl then directed the Emerald Guards to board the aircar with him, Kodhi, and the androids. As they were boarding, Kodhi beamed a message to the Emerald Palace that the Indigo Clan was returning Prince Karl to his family.

A couple of hours after Kodhi had delivered Karl to the Emerald Palace, Arenh and Kodhi left for the Crimson Palace with a fleet of warbots and troop carriers loaded with androids and Indigo guardsmen. When the Indigo fleet sat down in front of the Palace, several hundred of the Crimson Guard were standing at attention to greet them.

The Indigo troops quickly exited their ships and assumed a formation in front of their ships facing the Crimson Guard. The human warriors stood in front and the androids behind. Jonah waited near the Palace entrance to greet Arenh and Kodhi as they walked from their ship to meet him.

"Mikah has issued the decrees," Jonah told Arenh. "He's also summoned Adhalmar to the Crimson Palace and made it clear that we'll flatten the Emerald Palace if he doesn't comply. We're waiting for him now."

Adhalmar arrived shortly in a convoy of ground cars and armored trucks. The Emerald Lord and

Lady Katrina, his wife, emerged with four of the Emerald Guard who served as their personal bodyguards. Prince Karl followed them with his personal guards. The fleet of trucks behind them carried the storm troops who composed most of what was left of the Emerald army. They deployed quickly in what Arenh considered an extremely unwise show of force.

Kodhi sent half of the androids to form a shield in front of the Indigo and Crimson forces. He sent the remainder of the robots into head-on confrontation with the Emerald troops. The androids waded into the ranks of the Emerald forces with stun guns blazing. The Emerald troops who were able to return fire before being knocked down found their weapons hardly fazed their opponents. The androids methodically handcuffed and shackled the Emerald soldiers and laid them in rows on the ground. In less than a half hour, the entire Emerald military force had been incapacitated, including the personal guards of Adhalmar. The androids, however, didn't touch the personal guards of Prince Karl and Lady Katrina. Adhalmar appeared to notice this but said nothing.

Arenh could feel Adhalmar's confusion and fear. He wished there were a more merciful way to deal with the tyrant. When Arenh probed the mind of Katrina, however, he felt only coldness and hostility. "As I expected," he thought.

Arenh apologized to Lady Katrina and Prince Karl. He told them that no one appeared fatally wounded and assured them they weren't in danger. He intentionally didn't extend the same assurances to Adhalmar, but ordered Kodhi to arrest him and take him into the Palace. He escorted Katrina and Karl himself.

When they were standing before Mikah, Katrina spoke first.

"Your Majesty," she began, "I plead with you to spare me, my son, and my household. We are not parties to the treason of my husband. I petition you also to issue a decree of divorce to separate me from Lord Adhalmar immediately."

"Whore!" Adhalmar exploded. Kodhi, who was standing behind the Emerald Lord while Katrina was speaking, slapped him behind the head so hard he fell forward to the floor. Then Kodhi motioned two androids to help him stand up again. The machines continued to stand one on each side of him. Adhalmar appeared to have little fear for other men, but he was clearly terrified of the machines.

Kodhi said in a quiet voice, "You will refrain from speaking, sir, until you are asked a question or given permission to speak." Kodhi's eyes drifted over towards Arenh as he spoke. Arenh didn't want to encourage him to more violence, but he signaled his approval with a slight nod.

After a few seconds of uncomfortable silence, Mikah spoke. "Lady Katrina, your petition is granted in its entirety. Your household will be spared, and your divorce request is granted."

When Mikah spoke, Arenh was startled to feel Katrina's emotions. He recoiled at the depths of her hatred. He noticed Mikah felt the same negative emotions from her. But his reaction was different. A slight smile formed on his lips, and Arenh felt a coldness from him. He had never seen Mikah like this and was unsettled by it.

Mikah felt Arenh's concern and looked at him. "So sorry, my love," he thought to Arenh. Then aloud he said, "I hereby decree that the traitor Adhalmar has by his treason made himself unworthy to wear the Emerald Cloak and is hereby deprived of his royal title. The title is, however, at the same time conferred on his son, Prince Karl. Captain Kodhi, remove the Emerald Cloak from the traitor's shoulders and hand it to me."

Kodhi released the clasp on the Emerald Cloak, removed it from Adhalmar's shoulders, and handed it to Mikah.

"Prince Karl," Mikah said. "Come forward." Karl obeyed.

Mikah stood and fastened the Cloak around Karl's shoulders. "Karl of the Emerald Clan," Mikah said, "in assuming the Cloak of your Clan, you assume authority over its lands and people. Do you swear to rule them with justice and wisdom?"

Karl dropped to one knee and said, "I do, Your Majesty."

"Rise, Lord Karl."

As Karl stood up, Katrina closed her eyes in what Arenh knew was an expression of disgust. He probed her memories and focused on one in particular of a time when she said to Adhalmar, "If you had only listened to me and killed the Indigo warlock's whelp when you had the chance."

Arenh's attention drifted from Katrina's memories to the sound of Mikah's voice. He was reading a decree in which he deprived Adhalmar of all entitlements, houses, lands, monies, and other possessions. He left him dependent on his son for the resources necessary to live.

After the Emerald Clan had departed, Mikah and Arenh flew to the Mountain with Jonah and Kodhi to discuss the events of the day. The two princes knew that their captains were not entirely pleased with the way they had dealt with Adhalmar's treason.

"By law," Jonah told Arenh, "he should have been executed. He murdered your father and attempted to murder you and Mikah. He abolished the Council and suspended the constitution. If we hadn't intervened, he would have killed most of the Crimson Clan. He should have died for any one of those offenses!"

"I agree with Jonah," Kodhi told them. "I wish we had discussed this before the hearing."

"We knew of what your advice would be," Arenh replied. "And we seriously considered ordering a public execution for Adhalmar. But violence breeds violence, and there's no end to it. Enough is enough. At some point, we have to stop. If our position were less secure, we would have to kill Adhalmar. But we're strong enough now to spare him and still be sure he causes no more harm."

Kodhi was unconvinced. "I've always assumed the whole point of getting more power is to use it. If you spare the snake, it will find a way to strike again in the future." Then he quickly added, as if to soften his disagreement, "But I liked the way you turned Karl and his mother against Adhalmar. That was smart."

"That was actually my idea," Mikah said. "Arenh's not devious enough to think of anything like that."

Arenh grabbed Mikah by the hair and pulled his head back to expose his neck while slowly drawing his extended forefinger across Mikah's throat.

"On second thought," Mikah said, "Maybe it *was* Arenh's idea."

They all laughed as Mikah shook his head and smoothed his hair back into place. But Jonah said, "I hope we're still laughing at this time next year. Adhalmar still has a lot of influence. Many among the nobility and the merchants are just as evil as he is. They'll continue to support him."

"Yes," Kodhi predicted, "I bet we'll eventually have to destroy the Emerald Clan entirely, or they will destroy us."

The next morning, however, Adhalmar was found dead with a knife in his belly. Kodhi brought the news to Arenh. "They say it was suicide. Maybe I was wrong in my prediction."

"I wouldn't assume anything. Lady Katrina had more to fear from Adhalmar regaining power than we did."

"You think she had him offed?"

"I think she's capable of it," Arenh sighed. "We may soon discover we should have removed her from the picture along with Adhalmar." He had no idea of how prophetic that statement would prove to be.

Chapter 10—Meeting the Ourdhu

MIKAH arrived in the Mountain by aircar not long after Kodhi had informed Arenh of Adhalmar's demise. He and Arenh sat in meditation in the zendo for the remainder of the day. Mikah decided to have the evening meal with Arenh and to spend the night in the Mountain.

When they were having tea after dinner, Arenh told Mikah he had heard of a linguistic anthropologist in the Crimson Clan who had been studying the Ourdhu language.

"Yes, her name is Myra," Mikah told him.

"How fluent is she in their language?"

"She's not. But I'm sure Myra knows more about it than anyone else in the clans. She sent me copies of a small lexicon and a grammar she wrote."

"Would you be willing to detail her to the Mountain for as long as the Ourdhu are our guests?"

"She's a member of the Academy of Sciences, so she makes her own decisions about things like that. But I predict she'll be begging your permission to enter the Mountain when she learns the Ourdhu are here."

"Good. Invite her on my behalf to join us in the Mountain to interview the Ourdhu. I think I may be able to sense some of their thoughts. But even if I do, I have no way to talk to them."

"As good as done," Mikah said.

"Kodhi has kept the Ourdhu warriors under continuous observation," Arenh explained, "and he believes that one of the wounded is their chief. This guy was clinically as dead as you were before regeneration. He appears to be the same age we are, so he's likely to be the chief for a long time to come, all the more so considering the effects of regeneration. This may be an opportunity to end the conflict between us and the Ourdhu. There's no reason for us to be at war that I can see. If there was a reason at one time, there isn't anymore."

"To end it would certainly be good for *us*, but even better for *them*, I think," Mikah agreed.

Later the next day, after Mikah had returned to the Palace, an armored aircar bearing the Crimson shield entered Hangar Bay Three on the west side of the Mountain, and Myra stepped out. She appeared to be in her forties with graying blonde hair that was thick, curly, and cut close to her head. She wore a mid-thigh crimson chiton with a gold belt—a style usually regarded as male attire—and a floor-length white cloak trimmed in crimson and gold. She requested an audience with Arenh in a formal manner. The guardsman on duty was expecting her and directed her to Arenh's office immediately.

When she entered Arenh's office, he noticed she had what appeared to be her overnight bag with her. "A very good sign," he thought.

Arenh explained to the anthropologist how the Ourdhu had come to be in the Mountain and that they suspected one of them was the chief.

Myra could scarcely contain her excitement. She requested another anthropologist be allowed to join her, a man named Branunh. "He's a social anthropologist," she explained. Arenh was pleased to grant her request.

"Very good," Myra said. "I took the liberty of bringing him with me. He's waiting in the aircar."

"You did well," Arenh told her. "I'll accompany you back to the car to meet him."

After Arenh had met Branunh, he led the two scientists to the quarters of the Ourdhu. Myra and Branunh stared at their surroundings in awe. House-cleaning bots were crawling around on the floors like giant metal insects and server bots floated through the corridors like mini-aircars with eyes and arms. But the androids appeared to interest them most. The androids looked like helmeted human beings in full body armor. They were everywhere and watched everything. Arenh knew they could be unnerving for someone not accustomed to them, but the two anthropologists seemed more fascinated than fearful.

When they reached the small cavern where the Ourdhu were being held, they found Kodhi waiting for them. His neural link to the androids had informed him they were coming.

Arenh asked Myra if she could introduce him to the man they thought was the Ourdhu chief.

"We may need to use our automated translators," she answered, "but I'm confident we can do it."

Kodhi and his guards brought the chief in. He was wearing a brown cloth kilt, sandals, and nothing else but a beard and very long hair. He immediately prostrated himself before Arenh. Arenh knelt down beside him and motioned for him to stand.

The chief stood as Arenh requested, but looked confused. He began to speak, but Arenh could pick up only a few of his thoughts—an image of a man in chains, an image of a man on a throne—but none of it made sense.

Arenh looked to Myra and Branunh for help. They conferred a moment and consulted their machines, which had recorded and analyzed what the Ourdhu had said.

"He says his name is Orokh, chief of the Ourdhu," Myra said, "and we believe that he's offering to become your slave if you will free the other Ourdhu you are holding as prisoners."

Orokh seemed to realize that Myra could understand him, so he talked to her instead of Arenh and went on at length.

After Myra and Branunh had spent a few minutes analyzing and translating, Branunh said, "He wishes to thank you for bringing him back from the dead. He wishes to thank you for healing his injured warriors. He says—and this part we aren't sure of—that if they had known the dwellers in the Mountain were gods, they would never have made war against them.

"Now the remainder of this is more certain," Branunh continued, "he says he and his warriors all by right owe their lives to the God of the Mountain.

But he says many have families who will not survive without them. That is why he asks that all be permitted to return to their homes. In exchange, he will become your slave, and all Ourdhu will take an oath to make no more war against the Mountain dwellers."

Branunh looked triumphant when he had finished.

"Thank you Branunh, and thank you Myra," Arenh said. "Now can you tell him that we are not gods, we are people just like him. Tell him they are not prisoners and that tomorrow morning we will transport them all back to their homes."

Myra and Branunh looked a little disappointed about the Ourdhu returning home the next morning, but they went to work conferring with their machines and with each other. Then they touched a final button, and the machine spoke with an artificial voice.

The chief was startled by the voice of the machine and was confused at first about where it came from. But as the meaning of the words began to dawn on him, he looked at Arenh and spoke again.

Myra didn't take so long to translate this time. "He expresses gratitude, swears the allegiance of the Ourdhu to you and vows that they will never make war against you again."

She then showed Arenh a picture she had pulled up on the computer display of two men. Each was grasping the other's right forearm with his right hand while placing his left hand on the other's right shoulder. "It means *we are brothers*," she assured him.

Arenh reached out and took Orokh's right forearm. The Chief had a questioning look on his face for a moment, and then smiled. He grasped Arenh's forearm, and each of them placed his left hand on the other's right shoulder.

Orokh then said something which Myra translated as "This is a wonderful (or glorious or joyful or holy) day."

"It could mean any or all of those things," she explained.

Arenh gave Myra and Branunh permission to remain with Kodhi's guards in the quarters of the Ourdhu. Arenh told Kodhi that he would go with Kodhi's guards when they transported the Ourdhu back to their home.

Kodhi replied, "Then I will go also."

Arenh slept soundly that night. And early the next morning he skipped the first meal and went directly to the quarters of the Ourdhu. They were being taken out in groups to waiting airborne carriers. It was taking a little longer than expected, Kodhi explained to him, because the Ourdhu were reluctant to enter the carriers until Orokh ordered them to do so. But when he commanded each group to enter, they complied. Orokh clearly trusted his new brother.

The carriers flew with a small fleet of warbots towards one of the Ourdhu villages in the valley, the one pointed out by Orokh. Myra and Branunh accompanied them. The two anthropologists had persuaded Arenh they might be needed as

70

interpreters, but they were obviously motivated more by the opportunity to visit an Ourdhu village.

They could see the entire village from the air as they approached it, a collection of neat one-story structures, some of wood and some of stone, surrounded by a low stone fence that was no higher than a man's waist. As the troop carriers and warbots landed on the outskirts of the village, there was a great commotion inside. Arenh had expected this. He had his hand on Orokh's shoulder. And the moment the fleet touched ground, Arenh touched the Amulet.

When Orokh found himself standing on the ground with Arenh in front of the fleet without having moved, he grabbed Arenh's arm tightly out of shock. But he recovered quickly and shouted something to his people, which Myra later translated as, "Have no fear—the gods are our friends." When the Ourdhu warriors began to emerge from the carriers, their families came running from the village to embrace them.

Arenh touched the Amulet and relocated himself in the carrier. He ordered Kodhi to lift off, and the fleet started to rise. Orokh, who had been distracted by the greetings of his wife and children, looked up at the departing carriers and saluted with his right fist against his abdomen.

"They believe that compassion and kindness are located in the bowels," Myra explained.

"Seems I recall," Arenh said, "that some ancient cultures on Earth thought the same thing."

"Yes," Branunh agreed, "while others located such emotions in the heart."

"I was shocked," Myra said, "when you disappeared with Orokh and reappeared before the village. My concern is that now the Ourdhu won't likely be convinced that we're people like them. I myself could easily believe you're a god. Or perhaps a wizard, which many in the City believe. But I know there's some rational explanation."

"I should have consulted with you and Branunh before doing what I did," Arenh said, "but then, I would have had much to explain."

"Things I'm sure he's not going to explain," Myra thought and which Arenh sensed as she thought it.

"I decided," Arenh continued, "that it wouldn't likely hurt the Ourdhu to idealize us as long as they see the gods as being kind and loving beings. Of course, we'll have to take care—for their welfare—to hide the sad reality of the other side of our nature.

"One thing we have going for us is that Orokh is very intelligent. Though he may for his own reasons have told his people we are gods, I could tell by the way he grasped my arm that he knew I was flesh and blood like him."

Arenh couldn't let them know that he had also shared some of Orokh's thoughts. "We keep as many secrets from our own people," he thought, "as we do from the Ourdhu."

Chapter 11—Making a baby

D URING the weeks following the return of the Ourdhu to their home, Mikah and Arenh spent their days rebuilding the institutions of democracy that Adhalmar had destroyed. They spent most of their nights together, though Mikah needed occasionally to spend the night with Leah. If the two men spent one night in Mikah's chamber, they would spend the next night they could be together in Arenh's.

One morning in Arenh's apartment, Mikah said, "Leah would like for you to join us for dinner this evening."

Arenh picked up on some confusing thoughts from Mikah and had the impression he had suppressed a thought. But he often did the same thing, so he thought no more about it.

"You'll be going to the Palace anyway to spend the night with me," Mikah continued, "so just arrive a few hours early."

Arenh agreed. He traveled by aircar to the Palace that evening because he was accompanied by Kodhi and two of his guards. Kodhi had said he and Jonah planned a meeting that night. So Arenh wasn't surprised to find Jonah and two of the Crimson Guards waiting for them at the Palace.

Jonah bowed to Arenh in a playful way. "My Lord, we are honored!" he said affectionately.

"I'm sure you are," Arenh joked. He noticed Jonah and Kodhi were exchanging knowing looks, as though they knew something he didn't. He resisted an inclination to probe their thoughts more deeply. Jonah led him to the dining chamber and opened the door for him.

As Arenh entered, he noticed the room had marble floors, thick varnished wood paneling that soared upwards for 20 feet, and an artfully painted ceiling—nothing like the simple unpretentious rooms within the Mountain.

Mikah was mixing drinks at a tastefully ornate sideboard against the wall. The Queen was already seated at the table.

Leah looked much different than when Arenh had seen her in the Mountain after the battle with Adhalmar. She was wearing a white floor-length chiton with a crimson belt. The only jewelry she wore was the clasp that held her hair up. She wore no makeup. She needed none.

Leah extended her hand. Arenh took it and kissed it. "Good evening, Your Majesty!"

Leah nodded and smiled. "I guess I set the tone by lifting my hand like that," she apologized. "But it wasn't the tone I intended to set. Let's dispense with the formalities."

Arenh noticed that as she turned, her right breast was fully exposed from the side. "Enough to turn a lover of men to women," he thought. He looked away just in time to see Mikah grin. Arenh blushed when he realized that Mikah had read his thoughts.

"So good to see you!" Mikah said as he crossed the room. He kissed Arenh on the lips for what seemed to Arenh a bit longer than was appropriate. "Please sit down."

Arenh's discomfort was apparent as he obeyed.

"Arenh," Leah said, "the first time I saw you was here in the Palace during your teens. Even then you were a cutie pie. But I have to say, you've grown into a magnificent specimen of the male gender."

"Thank you, ma'am," Arenh said nervously and blushed again.

Arenh remembered that Leah was ten years older than him and Mikah. The Spacenglish dialect of the colonists was permeated with Old Earth slang. So when the image of a cougar popped into Arenh's mind, Mikah strangled on his drink.

"Are you all right, my dear!?" Leah asked.

"Yes," Mikah replied a bit hoarsely, "just went down the wrong pipe."

Arenh began to relax a little. "You should be more careful," he said to Mikah. "People have *died* because of things like that."

Mikah looked at him as though he couldn't believe his ears. Then he coughed again and said, "Excuse me, I'll be right back."

When Mikah was out of the room, Leah got right to the point.

"I find you quite attractive, Arenh," she said matter-of-factly, "and I would enjoy having you join me in bed one night. Tonight, in fact, would be good."

Arenh was grateful he hadn't been taking a swallow of his drink at that moment, or he would surely have been strangling for breath along with Mikah.

"I don't know what to say, Leah," he managed. "You're one of the most beautiful women I've ever seen, but you know—as far as women are concerned—I'm a virgin. I've always been inclined towards men. I wouldn't know what to do if we were in bed together."

"Oh, you wouldn't need to know anything about that, my dear," she assured him. "I know quite enough for the both of us."

Arenh had to laugh.

"Let me be frank," she said.

He wondered what her word was for the way she had already been.

"There's a problem between me and Mikah."

"I see. But don't you think that an affair with me would just make things worse between you and Mikah?"

"Oh I'm not suggesting an affair, my dear," she quickly explained. "Not that I wouldn't enjoy that. I just know that you wouldn't. And even if you would, your loyalty to Mikah would prevent it."

He was really getting confused now.

"Mikah must produce an heir," she explained. "His dynasty comes to an end otherwise. There's not even a nephew to succeed him."

"Is he not fertile?" Arenh was genuinely concerned.

"God I hope he's not shooting blanks! But we'll never find out as long as his noodle is limp." She didn't appear concerned about mixing metaphors.

Unfortunately, Arenh was taking a sip of his drink at that point and just managed to keep from spraying it over the table.

"I see," he said. And when he had recovered sufficiently, he continued. "And how do I fit in with respect to this problem?"

"Well, he doesn't have the limp noodle problem with you does he?" she asked with a hopeful tone.

"Oh no," Arenh assured her. "Not at all."

"Wonderful! So would you consider joining us in bed to, uh, *inspire* him?"

"I— I don't know," Arenh stammered. "This is something I've never thought of before."

"Well, it's either you or one of the young men of the guards. He's really taken with your captain. What's his name— Kodhi?"

"Oh no!" Arenh found himself protesting. "I would certainly prefer it to be me!"

"I thought you would feel that way," she said with a smile.

Arenh thought, "This woman is a force to be taken seriously."

Mikah entered the room at that point and said aloud in response to Arenh's thought, "Tell me about it."

"Tell you about what, dear?" Leah asked.

"Oh nothing," Mikah mumbled. "Just talking to myself."

"Well," she said to Mikah, "you'll be pleased to know that Arenh has agreed to help us. And I'm sure Jonah will be relieved too."

"Jonah!?" Arenh exclaimed. "Who all knows about this?"

"You were the last to know," Mikah confessed. "It was Jonah's idea, but Kodhi was the one who talked to me about it first."

"Well, let's eat dinner," Leah interrupted. She signaled with a small bell on the table, and servers began to bring in platters of food.

The Royal Family used human servers. Arenh had grown accustomed to server bots. He had always felt uncomfortable with other human beings waiting on him. As they came in, he acknowledged each one with eye contact and a nod or a smile. Some of them responded in kind, and others appeared not to know how to respond.

"I have an appointment later, something that came up at the last minute," Leah told them. "It won't take long. I suggest the two of you retire to Mikah's chamber after we eat, and I'll join you later."

Arenh thought, "She doesn't waste any time." He noticed Mikah looking at him with amusement.

The meal was much different from the simple diet to which Arenh was accustomed. The Royal Family of the Crimson Clan was renowned for its vegetarian cuisine. They had centuries earlier joined the Indigo Clan in the abolition of slaughter, though most of the Crimson Clan remained as carnivorous as the Emerald and were, in fact, among the best customers of the Emerald meat merchants. The Royal family, however, had always remained true, at least in their diet, to the ethical ideal of *ahimsa*.

The servers brought in several baked vegetable casseroles, bowls of stir-fried vegetable delicacies, plates of roasted mushrooms and meat analogs, pastries and pies of several kinds, a variety of toasted nuts, and platters of fruit and cheese.

"Far more than the three of us could eat in a week," Arenh thought. Mikah glanced at him apologetically.

After they had eaten and Leah had left, Mikah invited Arenh to his bed chamber. On the way, they passed Jonah and Kodhi. Mikah gave them the thumbs up. They smiled, and Arenh blushed. He wondered silently if there were some genetic engineering trick that could prevent that.

Mikah said aloud, "It's cute. Everybody loves it."

After the two of them were lying in bed together, Mikah forbade any intimacy until Leah joined them. That soon created a burning desire in Arenh, which was about to derange him. The prohibition appeared to be producing the same effect in Mikah. But Mikah insisted they must not touch, so Arenh thought to distract himself with conversation.

"Why didn't you ask me to do this yourself?" he asked Mikah.

"I was afraid to, I guess," Mikah replied. "Also they seem to have had more difficulty convincing me this was a good idea than you."

"By *they,* I assume you mean Leah and Jonah?"

"Yes. And Kodhi."

Arenh stared in amazement. "What were you afraid of?"

"I think I was mostly concerned that you wouldn't have the same problem with Leah that I do. To secure an heir to the Cloak isn't the only reason she wants you in bed with her, I assure you."

"I understand," Arenh said. "It's only natural that a man doesn't want to share his wife—even with his best friend."

"No, sweet Arenh," Mikah replied, "You don't understand at all. I share my wife with men I don't even know. The problem is sharing my best friend with my wife!"

Arenh couldn't help but smile and extended his hand to touch Mikah's chest.

"Don't!" Mikah ordered. "It's a slippery slope I'm on. One little touch and the night's over for me!"

Arenh laughed. "Had it occurred to you that she could have a baby by one of her boy toys and that you could adopt the child as your own?"

"Neither Leah nor I would ever permit that. She's careful to practice contraception. We did consider that you might father a child with Leah, and I would treat him as my own. That would please me. But you're dark. Leah and I are both fair. The genetics would surely betray us."

"Did you consider being a sperm donor for artificial insemination? I could've helped you collect your little baby seeds."

"That was my first idea. But Leah wouldn't hear of it. She says a baby should be conceived with love."

"She has something there. But I think artificial insemination can be done with love. Just like the old fashioned way can be done without love."

They lay in bed together silently for what seemed a very long time to Arenh while the hormones raged in his body. His mindlink with Mikah told him that he also was approaching the point that would make this whole effort pointless unless Leah arrived soon.

Fortunately, Leah arrived a few minutes later and entered the chamber without knocking. Arenh got out of bed. And with no one saying anything, Leah dropped her chiton to the floor and lay down beside Mikah. Then Arenh returned to bed on her other side.

"I'm happy to see," she said softly as she stared first at Mikah's crotch and then at Arenh's, "that no one's having the limp noodle problem tonight." As she said it, she looked again at Mikah with a look he had never seen before, at least not for him.

"Oh I think this is going to work," Mikah said as he turned on his side and pulled her towards him.

Arenh lay beside them a few minutes and then realized he didn't exist anymore as far as the royal couple was concerned. "They're well on their way to making a baby," he thought. So he quietly slipped out of bed. He retrieved the Indigo Cloak from a chair and threw it over his shoulder. As he opened the door to leave, he looked down with annoyance at his erection.

"Whatta guy!" someone said. He looked up to see Jonah and Kodhi standing outside the bed chamber. The remark had come from Jonah.

Arenh swung the Cloak around quickly to cover himself. And, of course, he blushed as usual.

"I would ask what's up," Kodhi said, "but that's obvious."

"That's enough, Kodhi!" Arenh said. But Kodhi pretended not to hear.

"I bet Her Majesty had some fun with that," he grinned.

"Never touched it," Arenh said. "Once she saw Mikah at full mast, she didn't know I was in the room. I think this whole story about erectile dysfunction was a hoax."

"Why would they pretend about something like that?" Jonah asked.

"They're kinky," Arenh muttered.

Both Kodhi and Jonah were struggling to keep from laughing out loud for fear of disturbing Mikah and Leah.

"I'm glad you two fellas are amused." Arenh said. "And Kodhi," he continued, "you'll have to find your own way home. I'm going *now*. I have to find a private place to take care of some personal needs."

"I would offer to help," Kodhi said, "but once a man experiences the joy of women, he loses interest in brotherly love."

"If you're trying to raise my anxiety about Mikah and me, you're succeeding," Arenh told him.

"I'm only teasing you, Arenh," Kodhi said in a pretense of apology. "Mikah is very much in love with you. I'm sure of it. Almost."

Jonah lost it and laughed out loud.

"You have a wicked streak in your soul, Captain Kodhi," Arenh said. And before either of the two soldiers could say anything in reply, he touched the Amulet and disappeared.

The morning after the ménage à trois that didn't quite happen, Arenh was awakened by a knock on his door. Mikah entered without waiting to be invited.

"Stay in the bed," Mikah said as he dropped his chlamys and crawled in bed beside Arenh. "Just came to thank you."

"There's nothing I wouldn't do for you, Mikah, though you did make it kind of hard."

"Kind of?"

"I'm being selfish." Arenh ignored the implied pun. "I'm happy for you and Leah."

"As I've told you before, Leah and I are dear friends. And sexual intimacy with a friend is very powerful as you know. But really it wouldn't have happened at all if I hadn't been so aroused by lying there with you before Leah came in. She and I planned it that way. But we never thought you would get jealous and leave. And I expected even less that you would get worried about our relationship.

"Jonah told me this morning about how Kodhi teased you last night," Mikah continued. "He can be an imp—a lovable, handsome imp, but still an imp."

"Kodhi meant no harm. And I don't think I was jealous," Arenh said. "I was happy to see you humping Leah as if there were no tomorrow. But I admit I got worried about you and me. I don't see how your relationship with Leah can change while our relationship stays the same. That's not the way things work. Everything's interconnected. What happens in one of our relationships affects them all in some way."

"Maybe so, but I don't buy the idea that you and I will be less close because Leah and I are closer. Had it occurred to you that you and I may be closer too?"

"I hadn't looked it that way."

They were both silent for a few moments. And then Arenh asked, "Do you think you succeeded in making a baby?"

"We'll know soon," Mikah said. "If not, well, you know, *if at first you don't succeed...*"

"Well, when we try again," Arenh said—and Mikah noticed he said *when* instead of *if*—"I'll stick around a bit longer. The next time I intend to get my turn with one of you."

"Or both?"

"You really are kinky, my friend," Arenh replied as he rolled over on Mikah and pretended to pin his shoulders to the bed.

"True," Mikah smiled. "But only with you."

Chapter 12—The indictment

A WEEK after the royal couple's attempt to ensure the survival of the Crimson dynasty, Leah's pregnancy test was positive. The fetus was confirmed a few days later to be male. Arenh was happy that Mikah would have an heir, but disappointed that he wouldn't get to share the same bed with Leah and Mikah for a while. Leah insisted on no sex until after the baby was born. During the weeks that followed, however, she often wanted Mikah to sleep with her and hold her. So Arenh spent fewer nights with Mikah.

"I hope you understand," Mikah said.

"She gets priority," Arenh assured him.

"She's like a different person," Mikah declared.

"I think she's happy now," Arenh told him. "She'll be a devoted mother for sure. And a devoted wife."

Mikah looked at Arenh with a worried expression. "You can't hide anything from me, Arenh. I can feel your sadness. You're still afraid you're going to lose me. But you're wrong. You'll see."

"I just need a little time to adjust to the new situation. I wonder, does Leah have a sister?"

"No," Mikah laughed. "Unless there's something Jonah's not telling us."

"I forget that Jonah's her brother."

"Yeah. There were just the two of them. They were born only a year apart, and they're very close."

In the months that followed, Arenh had less and less time with Mikah at night. But Mikah joined him often in the zendo for daily mind training and sometimes joined him working in the gardens.

In the last month of Leah's pregnancy, Arenh went to mind training alone one day because Mikah was preoccupied with business at the Palace. He returned to his apartment and had the evening meal early. He lay down on the sofa soon after eating and had fallen asleep when someone knocked on his door.

"Come in, Kodhi," he called out sleepily and then wished he hadn't said Kodhi's name.

But Kodhi didn't seem to notice. "Mikah asks that you come at once," he reported. "Something's happened." He appeared to be very agitated. "I'm not supposed to talk about it until we're with Mikah and Jonah," he said.

Arenh's first thought was that Leah was suffering complications with the pregnancy. He resisted the temptation to probe Kodhi's mind.

"Let's go then," Arenh said, without questioning him. He lifted his forearm as a signal for Kodhi to grasp it and touched the Amulet with his other hand. They were relocated in Mikah's office.

Mikah was seated at a table on which were a number of papers. Jonah was with him. Mikah shoved a document across the table to Arenh and said, "Read this."

Arenh read the document silently. It was a secret indictment against him issued by the High Council. It required Mikah to arrest him for the murder of Adhalmar.

"This is absurd!" Arenh exclaimed. He felt a rush of anger. He sat in silence as he read the rest of the document, breathing in awareness of his anger and breathing out awareness of his fear until the emotions began to fade and his clarity of mind returned.

"No need to fear," Mikah reassured him. "I restored the Council by decree. I can dissolve the Council by decree."

"Adhalmar murdered your father, Arenh." Kodhi said. "Under the law, two of the Three Lords can remove the third for such an offense. You and Mikah had the right to execute him while he was still the Emerald Lord. But after the title passed to Karl, the decision was yours alone. You had the right to do it."

"I didn't kill him," Arenh said to Kodhi. "I don't understand what's happened to motivate this."

"A chambermaid testified she saw you appear in a hallway and then enter Adhalmar's room," Mikah answered. "She heard Adhalmar scream. Then she says you came out of the room into the hallway again and vanished."

"If I had killed Adhalmar, you can be sure there would be no witness," Arenh declared.

"I had an advocate present when her deposition was taken," Mikah said. "His questions and her answers are there on the table if you want to read them, but I'll summarize the main points. She can't really say she saw *you*. All she can say is that she saw someone appear and disappear, and she believes you are the only person who can do that. Also, he was wearing an indigo cloak that looked like yours. You are the only person who wears such a cloak, so she assumed the man had to be you. The advocate says she appeared to be very frightened."

"Did the advocate think she was being coerced?" Jonah asked.

"No, he thinks she believes she really saw Arenh, and now she's afraid he may kill her too."

"If the chambermaid really believes she saw Arenh, someone intended her to believe that," Kodhi said. "Who would have the power to make someone appear and disappear?"

"We don't know that anyone really appeared or disappeared," Mikah replied. "Maybe she was hallucinating."

"Maybe," Kodhi agreed. "In that case, who would have the power to cause and control her hallucinations?"

"The answer in either case," Arenh said, "is, of course, the Dreamers. But why would the Dreamers want to frame me? It doesn't make sense."

"When things don't make sense," Jonah said, "we're always lacking information. I believe things always make sense when we have all the facts."

The thought occurred to Arenh that the *more* facts he had about some things the *less* they made sense. Mikah sensed his thought and looked at him with a slight nod of agreement.

"Ordinarily the Council wouldn't issue an indictment until it held a hearing," Arenh said. "Yet that's what they did. There's something going on there we don't understand either."

"I have undercover operatives among the Council staff," Jonah said. "They haven't reported anything unusual. But sometimes they need a clue about what to look for. I'll see what they can dig up about the Council's motives for issuing the indictment without a hearing."

"I don't think they're motivated by love of Adhalmar," Kodhi said. "They have reason to hate him as much as anyone. The irony to me is that most everybody wanted him dead except for you, Arenh, and now they indict you for his murder without even a hearing. If the Council convicts you of this," he continued angrily, "I swear before God they will be sorry they did."

"I'm sure we have the military power to do whatever we wish," Arenh replied. "But whatever we do has to be lawful. Otherwise, we're no different from Adhalmar."

"You're in no way the same as Adhalmar," Kodhi said emphatically, "and neither is Mikah. If the Council does anything to harm either of you, they will pay with their lives, I promise you!"

"You both should know that I stand with Kodhi on this," Jonah said quietly.

"What you two say worries me more than the indictment," Arenh said, "even though I know you say it out of love for Mikah and me."

"The key to this seems to be the Dreamers," Mikah said. "We have to find out if they were involved in Adhalmar's death. And to do that, we need to find out what they are and what they're up to."

"I agree," Arenh replied. "But there won't be much opportunity for me to help with that. The indictment *requires* you, Mikah, to place me under arrest."

"I'm not going to do that, Arenh. I've instructed our advocates to research the legality of the indictment since it was issued without a hearing. Meanwhile, I've advised the Council that the indictment is suspended until the investigation into its legality is completed. Of course, they're crying foul."

"Thank you, Mikah. And thank you Jonah and Kodhi for standing by me." Arenh remembered that he and Mikah were supposed to spend the night together in the Mountain, but he really needed to sleep.

Mikah sensed his thoughts and said, "Why don't you go back to the Mountain and get some rest, and I'll see you here early in the morning."

"And you don't need to wait for me," Kodhi told him. "Jonah and I are having a late night planning session. We intend to be ready for any surprises."

"Okay," Arenh said. But he thought, "I hope they're not planning any surprises of their own."

Mikah picked up on the thought and looked at him with a smile. "Not to worry," he thought to Arenh, "I'll be with them." But aloud he said, "We love you."

Arenh simply nodded as he touched the Amulet and disappeared. He went to bed as soon as he was back in his own chamber. He had wanted to talk to his mother about the indictment, but the hour was too late to disturb her. Besides, he had always used sleep to cope with worry and confusion. Things often seemed to sort themselves out in his dreams, and he would awaken with new insights and a new perspective.

After Arenh had discovered that he and Mikah sometimes shared the same dream, he had begun to keep a dream diary. He made sure the book and a pen were on his bedside table before retiring. He woke up several times during the night to jot down key words that would jolt his memory the next morning of what he was dreaming about. Otherwise, he had found that he would forget most of his dreams.

Arenh got out of bed early the next morning. He dressed in his most modest tunic and fastened his cloak over his shoulders. His mother was a morning person like him. He sent a message to Donna to expect him shortly. He headed for his mother's apartment without waiting for an answer, knowing she would be out of bed already.

Donna was pleased to see him as usual. "Just a moment," she said, "while I make sure she's ready to receive company."

Arenh had realized years before that everyone was company to his mother, except perhaps Donna. He wondered sometimes about his mother's relationship with Donna but pushed such thoughts out of his head.

Donna reappeared and said, "She'll see you now, my dear."

When Arenh entered his mother's parlor, she apologized for not having tea ready.

"I'm the one who should apologize," Arenh said, "for dropping in on such short notice. And besides, as usual of late, I don't have time to stay for tea anyway."

"You promised on your last visit to stay longer next time," she reminded him.

"True," Arenh conceded. "But at least I did come properly dressed this time."

She smiled. "I didn't say you were dressed improperly the last time. I just saw that you weren't comfortable."

"I have bad news this time." He noticed a cloud come over her face. "The Council has indicted me for the murder of Adhalmar. Mikah has suspended it while our advocates determine its legality. Mikah thinks the law requires a hearing first."

"I thought you said bad news," his mother said with obvious relief. "I see this as a perfect opportunity to line them all up and eliminate them."

"You and Kodhi would make a formidable duo," Arenh laughed. "But we're more concerned about the Dreamers than the Council. As Mikah and I see it, we need to find out more about them and whether they were involved in what was going on."

"The way you said 'as Mikah and I see it' reminded me of the way your father would say 'as Edmunh and I see it'. As for the Dreamers, I'm sure they're involved with almost everything that happens on this planet."

"Do you remember if Father said anything just before his death that would give us a clue as to why the Dreamers didn't warn him of the ambush?"

"I wish he had. But he appeared to trust them right to the end. And so did Edmunh. I remember, though, that he and Edmunh had a difference over something just before his death. They seldom disagreed about anything. Ivanh was very hurt."

"You didn't suspect Edmunh?"

"No," she answered quickly. "He was devastated by Ivanh's death. I blamed the Dreamers for several years, but only because I felt they had abandoned Ivanh when he needed them most."

Arenh noticed that her eyes were moist. He leaned over and kissed her. "I need to return to Mikah and discuss all this with him, but I think he may be still asleep."

"Donna will send the servers with tea in a few minutes. Why don't you stay awhile longer and let Mikah sleep?"

"I'll do that," Arenh decided. "But enough of this talk about the Dreamers and the Council—let's talk about something really important, like what you've been reading lately or the music you've been listening to. We can invite Achilles to join us!"

"Achilles will love that," she laughed. "But you won't get a chance to say much. He'll try to kiss you every time you open your mouth!"

Chapter 13—Broken hearts

KODHI was a bit surprised when Arenh asked for an aircar and pilot to take him to the Crimson Palace. "Why not just *relocate* yourself—isn't that what you call it?" he inquired with a puzzled look.

"I need to check out a hunch on the way," Arenh said. Kodhi looked even more puzzled then, but quickly agreed to Arenh's request, which he understood was actually a polite order.

The pilot Kodhi assigned as Arenh's chauffeur was a woman about Arenh's age named Jenah.

"I wonder why you need a pilot," she told Arenh after introducing herself. "If you give the car your destination, it will take you there itself."

"Where we're going may require some unusual maneuvers. The robots don't do so well with anything unusual. I want you to take us by the north face of the Mountain peak on our way to the City. Pass as close to the peak as you consider safe and at minimum speed."

"As you command, My Lord," Jenah answered with obvious curiosity. She became even more curious in listening to Arenh's remarks when they cruised slowly by the peak as he had instructed.

"Just as I thought," he murmured once. "Exactly what I expected!" he said another time.

They arrived at the Crimson Palace about mid-morning. Arenh thanked the pilot and told her he would find his own way back. He entered the Palace and went straight to Mikah's quarters.

When the guard started to knock on the door to announce him, Arenh put his finger to his lips. "Is the Queen with him?" he whispered.

The guard shook her head no. She appeared nervous. Arenh whispered, "Thank you," and started to open the door, but the guard said, "Wait, My Lord, he's not—" Arenh stopped in the open door and stared— "alone," the guard finished her sentence weakly.

Arenh softly closed the door. "That's clearly not the Queen in bed with him."

"No, sir, that's Alinh, the other guard assigned to this station for the night."

"And what's your name please?"

"Lori, sir."

"Please do me a favor, Lori, and tell His Majesty after he wakes up that if he can find time for me in his social calendar today, I'll be waiting in my apartment."

"As you command, My Lord."

"No, that wasn't a command, Lori. It was a request for a personal favor. I don't command people to deliver a personal message like this."

"I'll see that he gets the message, sir. And meaning no disrespect to His Majesty, sir, but some men have balls for brains if you know what I mean."

Arenh felt pain in Lori's remark and realized that she was in love with Alinh. "She's as upset that he's in bed with Mikah as I am," he thought. "Yes, I know what you mean, Lori," he said softly. Then he touched the Amulet and—to Lori's amazement—disappeared.

Arenh waited an hour or so in his apartment after returning to the Mountain, expecting Mikah to knock on the door at any moment. When Mikah didn't appear, Arenh went to the zendo and sat in meditation until late afternoon and then returned to his apartment. He had begun to worry that all might not be well with his errant friend. But soon he heard the knock he had been expecting.

"You know you don't need to knock, Mikah," he called out. "And I wish you could say the same to me," he thought to himself or intended to think to himself, though Mikah picked up on it.

Mikah walked in with his head down. "You won't ever need to knock on my door again, Arenh. You'll never find anyone in my bed but me, or maybe me and Leah. And if that happens, both of us will be happy for you to join us. I know words mean nothing right now, but I'm truly sorry. I would give anything to turn the clock back and not do what I did."

"Alinh is quite beautiful," Arenh said. "If he were to shave his head and get a tan I could mistake him for Kodhi."

"He looks a lot like Kodhi. But that's the extent of the similarity. He's nothing like Kodhi really. He's irresponsible and inappropriately flirtatious. And for *me* to think he's inappropriate, you know he must really get out of line. He's been trying to catch my eye for some time, and I guess I encouraged him without intending to. Somehow he manipulated Jonah into assigning him to guard duty in the Palace. I woke up a few hours before daylight to find him standing at the end of the bed playing with himself. The games he plays could have cost him his life several centuries ago."

"The games he plays could cost him his life *today*," Arenh said, not realizing how his remark could be interpreted.

Mikah looked at him in surprise.

"What I mean," Arenh quickly explained, "is that sexual indiscretion with people who have the power to make you disappear after they've had their fun is like flirting with death."

"Well his life isn't in danger because of this, but his job is. That's why I'm so late getting here to see you. It turns out the other guard who was on duty in the palace last night is his girlfriend."

"Lori," Arenh said.

"Yes, Lori. She told me about your visit when she delivered your message. That was after she reported Alinh absent from his duty station. He and I slept late because we got so little sleep the night before. I guess her patience ran out and her anger took over.

"Jonah ordered Alinh arrested and hauled in for court-martial. I had to go to Jonah and explain what happened. I was really embarrassed telling Jonah about this, and you know I don't get embarrassed easily. I could feel his disappointment in me, even though he loves me so much he tried to hide it."

"What about Alinh?"

"He wasn't discharged, but he had to accept a demotion. And a period of probation. I guess I'm afraid that I'm facing something similar from you."

"You don't think I'll discharge you, huh?"

"I hope not."

Arenh smiled. "Don't worry my love. It'll be all right."

"You're not angry with me then?"

"Of course I'm angry. But I know the anger grows out of my hurt. And I feel hurt because I'm afraid."

"What have you got to be afraid of?"

"Not being good enough for you. Losing you. Being alone."

Mikah dropped his cloak and crawled in bed beside Arenh. "You have to know better than that. You haven't any reason to be afraid of any of those things. And I promise you this won't happen again."

"Yes, I know. You'll quit tomorrow."

"I can't expect you to believe me right now. I've destroyed your trust. No one could love you more than I do, Arenh. I just have this weakness, you know. Anyway, I had to make sure you're okay. I was so worried about you last night. I know I asked you to come to the Palace this morning, but I really intended to get up early and get to your apartment before you got out of bed."

"I've never doubted your good intentions, Mikah. But in your little book of *Sayings from Old Earth*, you'll find one somewhere about *the road to hell...*"

"Yeah, I know. You were already upset about the indictment. I guess I made things a helluva lot worse."

"Actually, I woke up this morning with a new perspective about the indictment. And a long visit with my mother also left me feeling better."

"Mothers do that, at least most of the time. I still miss my mother."

"I don't remember her. She must have died when you were very young."

"I was nine or ten years old, a few years before I met you. I was totally lost when she died. And I didn't really find myself again until I found you."

"How did she die?"

"A rare kind of leukemia. Now we would just take her to the bio-regenerator and all would be well."

There was such sadness in Mikah's voice that even without their mindlink, Arenh would have felt it. He put his hand on Mikah's hand and asked, "Do you remember the book of short poems that we found in the archives years ago? I can't remember the poet's name."

"Dickinson. I've memorized a lot of Miss D's poems."

"There's one in that book with a line that goes, '*They say that time assuages—but time never did assuage*'. Do you remember?"

"Better than you do," Mikah laughed. "The '*but*' isn't in there."

"My apologies to Miss D," Arenh smiled.

"I think she was right," Mikah said, "but I wonder if she really understood *why* time doesn't

99

assuage our pain. I really don't want the pain of losing my mother to go away. I hold on to it. I'm afraid I might forget her if I let it go. And I will never forget her."

"I think you're right. There are some memories that are too precious to let go, no matter how painful they are."

"You haven't eaten yet, have you?" Mikah asked in a more cheerful tone.

"Not yet."

"Why don't you join me? Let's go back to the Palace—the quick way. I know it's late in the day to do it, but I'll order the green gunpowder tea. I need the kick."

"Yeah, you don't look like you had much sleep last night and probably not much this morning either." Arenh regretted the remark immediately. "I could use some strong tea myself. I had tea early today with Mother, but her tea reminds me of jasmine-flavored water."

"Let's go then," Mikah said. He stood up and motioned for Arenh to embrace him chest to chest as they often did when they used the Amulet. But instead, Arenh just put one hand on Mikah's shoulder and touched the Amulet with the other. They were instantly in Mikah's chamber. Mikah appeared to be disappointed and worried. Arenh noticed, but pretended he didn't.

Chapter 14—The invitation

AFTER Mikah had ordered food and the gunpowder tea he had promised, Arenh said, "You remember I told you once that I thought the Dreamers must live, if that's the proper word, in a hidden cavern near the peak of the Mountain?"

Mikah nodded yes.

"Well the more I've thought about it, the more certain I've become. And I have an idea of a way into the Dreamers' abode. I had a dream last night of an opening in the Mountain on the north face of the peak. That area is off all the standard air lanes of the airborne vehicles. I had never seen this face of the peak.

"But I asked one of Kodhi's pilots to take a non-standard route to the City this morning that took us by the north side of the Mountain. There I saw the exact overhanging rock that I saw in my dream, and it was throwing the same deep shadow underneath.

"In the dream, I flew an aircar straight into this shadow. And just as I was sure the car was going to crash against the Mountain, the rock face of the peak dissolved into nothing. And the aircar entered the Mountain.

"It was a lucid dream," Arenh concluded. "I knew I was dreaming, and I knew that I had found the abode of the Dreamers. I think it was an invitation to visit them."

"Trouble is," Mikah said, "what if your dream was just an ordinary dream? Or what if the image of the overhang and the shadow were just images planted in your mind by the Dreamers to trick you into smashing yourself into a wall of solid rock?"

"I think I have to risk it."

"I know how you are when you're determined to do something," Mikah sighed. "I know it's pointless to object. You're not going to listen to me. So I hope you'll at least be open to my suggestions about *how* to do this."

"Yes, of course," Arenh assured him.

"There may be a way to reduce the risk. We could use an aircar as a lead vehicle. If it crashed into the wall, we would be in a second aircar that could instantly change our trajectory to one that would take us up and away from the peak instead of crashing us into it."

"I have two problems with that," Arenh replied.

"Okay, first problem first."

"First, what's this about *us*? I haven't said anything about *us*. We can't risk both our lives. And we certainly can't risk your life until your son is born and is old enough to take your place."

"I've already appointed you as regent," Mikah replied, "in case I disappear before junior is old enough to wear the Cloak. If you're not around either, then the regency will fall to a triumvirate of

Leah, Jonah, and Kodhi. No one is indispensable. So let's hear problem number two."

"Okay. The memories of the AI modules inside the aircars aren't of the same variety and depth as the artificial brains of the androids. But they are essentially the same technology. The memories they store are unique, and collectively they provide a unique perspective on the world similar to that of a human personality. I can't direct one of them to sacrifice itself for me, even though it would do it without hesitation."

"Yes I know. Their brains are built around a core of human brain cells—yours, in fact. But there may be a work-around for this problem. The core of cloned cells is identical in each of the robotic units, isn't it?"

"They start out that way, yes."

"Then shortly before this mission, we'll download the memory of the lead aircar into a storage unit. If the lead aircar crashes into the Mountain, we'll restore its memories to a new aircar. That way the one that's destroyed doesn't risk losing more than a few minutes of memories."

"Okay," Arenh conceded. "We'll do it your way."

"I think you should get the ball rolling right away," Mikah told him. "But I think we need to be clear about what we hope to accomplish by this. Do you want to destroy the Dreamers?"

"Oh no! I wouldn't want to do that even if we could. We need the Dreamers. And I think they need us, too, though I don't understand why. I want to do exactly what you suggested yesterday—find out if the Dreamers were involved in framing me for the murder of Adhalmar and also to learn more about them, what they are and what they're up to."

"You've thought this through," Mikah said. "And I see how important it is. So as long as I'm with you, I'm okay with it."

The servers knocked on the door and then entered with the evening meal and the tea Mikah had ordered.

"There's one other thing," Arenh told him after the servers had left and they had begun to eat. "I believe based on something my mother said this morning that your father and mine were very close, as though they shared the same viewpoint on many things. I think they were mindlinked like we are. The thing that most concerned me was what she said about a disagreement they had just before my father's death. I believe their mindlink was broken."

"You believe there's a connection between the mindlink being broken and your father's failure to foresee the ambush?"

"Yes. I think the Dreamers may be able to link more powerfully with our minds when we're mindlinked with each other than when we aren't— maybe because we're so much more limited as individuals. It's as though our mental powers are multiplied when our minds are linked."

"Like the whole is more than the sum of its parts," Mikah observed.

"Something like that, though it reminds me more of what happens when electrons pair up in a supercurrent."

"I see where you're going. We get to depend on being connected to each other in this mysterious and wonderful way. Our sphere of awareness expands to the point that we may even have premonitions of things that haven't happened yet. But if the link between us is broken, our sphere of awareness could suddenly shrink. That could be fatal to somebody in the wrong circumstances, and we don't need a lot of guesses to know who."

"That's it," Arenh replied.

"I guess my misbehavior last night has put us both in danger," Mikah reflected. "This is about the worst time to have this coolness between us—right before we visit the Dreamers."

"My reaction to what you did is just as important as what you did. And we both know that the coolness is all my problem. I think you're right about one thing though. We need to get past this before we try to visit the Dreamers. And knowing that may influence when we make our visit. I suggest the day after tomorrow."

"And what do we do between now and then?"

"Tomorrow," Arenh answered, "I think we should spend the day together in the zendo. That always strengthens our mindlink, and it may give my mind a chance to settle down."

"Sounds good," Mikah agreed.

After they had finished eating and were having their tea, Mikah suggested that Arenh spend the night in the Palace. "We'll get up early," he said, "and go to the Mountain together."

"I love you, Mikah. But right now I still need a little more time to myself. I hope you understand."

"I understand," Mikah said quietly. "I still can't forgive myself either."

"Don't beat yourself up over this, my love. I don't know if Miss Dickinson would have agreed, but I think this is the kind of thing that time *does* assuage. I'll meet you early tomorrow in the zendo. Sleep well."

Arenh touched the Amulet and disappeared before Mikah could say anything else. He regretted immediately that he had left so abruptly. As he got into bed, he thought about going back but decided against it. He really did need to be alone awhile. But he knew Mikah was in pain, and he wondered if he were unconsciously trying to hurt him. "I hope not. But if I am, that's worse than what he did," he thought as he drifted into sleep.

Mikah, meanwhile, lay awake, unable to sleep. He thought of joining Leah in her bed, but decided against it. He couldn't tell her what he had done. And the fact that he was afraid to tell her gave rise to a bit of resentment. "Now that she's turned into the perfect little wife and mother," he thought, "she would be more upset with me than Arenh is." But he knew that even Leah wouldn't be as upset with him as he was with himself. He had never felt so alone, even during the years when he wasn't able to see Arenh.

Chapter 15—Time to prepare

WHEN Arenh arrived at the zendo early the next morning, Mikah was already there. They spent most of the day together in mind training and shared the evening meal in Arenh's apartment.

"During the last few months," Arenh said, after they had finished eating, "you seem to have taken to Indigo mind training like it's natural for you."

"The training has a familiar feel to it, a feeling like I've done this before. I think our mindlink makes it easier for me."

"I think training with someone else is always easier than doing it alone, even without a mindlink," Arenh said.

"I think the mindlink between us continues to get stronger, and I'm happy for that," Mikah told him. "But I worry about it too. Sometimes I'm afraid that if I don't hold on to my own feelings and opinions I could lose my identity."

"I believe expanded consciousness involves looking at things from multiple viewpoints," Arenh replied. "If we blend our different perspectives into one way of looking at things, we lose a lot that's unique and precious, just as we would if one of us imposed his viewpoint on the other. Either way, it's as though we let only one flower bloom in the garden. I remember a saying from Old Earth—'*Let a hundred flowers bloom*'."

"That's a beautiful saying," Mikah said. "It could refer to more than just opinions and ideas. I could think of my love for you and my love for Leah as two beautiful flowers."

"Yes, I know," Arenh replied. "And I want both of them to bloom forever. But there's an old enemy who whispers from a dark corner in my mind, 'He may grow to love her more, and he may not want you anymore'."

"I could never love anyone more than I love you, Arenh. If you could just be sure of that, there wouldn't be any more dark corners in your mind." Mikah leaned over and kissed him on the cheek. "What do say about going to bed early tonight? We want to be sure to get enough sleep. We have to be our best for our visit to the Dreamers tomorrow."

"It's too early for sleep now."

"Yeah," Mikah grinned. "But we may not fall asleep right away."

"You're horny again."

"Not really. I'm just worried sick that you can't forgive me, and touching you is the only way I can be sure you have."

"I've forgiven you," Arenh assured him. "Please believe me."

"I believe you believe that. You can be one of the most convincing liars I've ever met because you believe your own lies. But when we're in bed, your body tells the truth."

"But what truth is my body telling you? Had it occurred to you I could be wondering who else you've been in bed with?"

"You can read my mind, my friend. Probe my memories if you need to," Mikah replied. "Except for that time with Alinh and when you and Leah and I were together, I haven't been sexual with anyone but you since you came back into my life.

"Leah and I sleep together, and we're close. But as you know, she doesn't permit anything sexual since she's pregnant. That wouldn't have bothered me in the past. But just lying there with her now and being forbidden to— Well, you can imagine what that does to me."

"Yeah, I can imagine," Arenh grinned as he put his arm around Mikah's shoulders and pulled him into a hug.

After a few moments, Mikah said sadly, "No, Arenh." He gently pushed Arenh away. "Something doesn't feel right. I can tell by the way you touch me."

Arenh looked concerned. "Maybe it's because Leah is your mate now, Mikah—not just in name but in fact. She loves you very much, and you've always loved her. You just couldn't be sexual with her in the past. Now you can. So maybe the time has come to cool things between us physically."

"That's a crock, Arenh! You know that's not what's wrong! This has nothing to do with Leah. You're punishing me for what I did with Alinh. But what I did, I did out of weakness. I had no intention of hurting you. And I know you don't want to hurt me—even though you are. You want to forgive me, but really you can't. So you withhold a part of yourself. You just can't help it."

Arenh was stunned. Mikah had never spoken to him before with such bluntness and force.

"Whoever said the truth never hurts was terribly misinformed," Arenh smiled with a wounded look. "You have a knack, my friend, for cutting right to the core of a problem. You're right, of course. I can fool myself. But how can I fool you? I've just drawn another circle around me—one I don't even let you enter. I don't want that to happen. But I don't know how to stop it."

Mikah put his hand on Arenh's. "How can you say you don't know? You practice it every time you're in the zendo. '*Breathe awareness in, and breathe attention out.*' And what's the second line?"

"Yes, I know," Arenh replied. '*Let awareness deepen into understanding, and let attention deepen into love.*' It seems simple, doesn't it? But after a lifetime of training, it's still not easy."

"Well I think you're still turned on by me," Mikah said. "I got that right, didn't I?"

"Yeah," Arenh laughed. "You got that right. I don't think you need to read minds to see that."

"And I think you still care for me. Right?"

"I would die for you."

"Well, why can't we get past this then?"

"I've always indulged in a romantic ideal," Arenh replied. "I've never had eyes for anyone but you. But you're different. I think your way of looking at things is more realistic in a way."

"I admit I slept around a little during the years I couldn't see you," Mikah confessed. "But I hope you

110

can understand that I didn't make love to any of those people. I just had sex with them. Same thing with Alinh. But you—it's different with you. I make love to you. Because I love you. And I have to be honest, even if it upsets you, I made love to Leah that night the three of us were together. And I want to do it again. I wish you two could love each other the way I love you both."

"I'm open to that happening," Arenh said. "I hope it will. I'm quite taken with Leah. So if it can happen with anybody, it can happen with her. But we have to be sure that's what *she* wants. I think motherhood has worked some changes in her. She wants you to lie next to her and hold her at night. She doesn't need me to do that. I know she's attracted to me physically. But I'm not her soulmate like you are."

"That's the whole thing, isn't it? I have two soulmates. You and Leah have only one."

"Yeah, I think that's it," Arenh agreed. "But she and I have the same one. So that helps. But now, let's stop talking for a while."

"You need to sleep?"

"No. I just find it hard to talk to a guy when I have my tongue in his mouth."

"Oh," Mikah grinned. "Well, that does take practice."

"You just don't know when to shut up, do you?" Arenh grasped Mikah's head in both hands and kissed him firmly on the lips.

A couple of hours later, they said good night. And when they said good morning the next day, the sun was just rising. Without telling anyone where they were going, an omission that would have unexpected consequences, they left in an aircar for the north face of the peak with an empty aircar leading the way.

They arrived at the overhanging rock on the north side of the peak in a few minutes. Both cars hovered in the air a short distance from the peak for a few moments.

"What do you think they will look like?" Mikah asked.

"They could look like anything. They appeared to me once in the garden as a butterfly. Or they may take no form at all, as usual."

"Are you ready?" Mikah asked.

"You say the word."

Mikah gave the order to proceed, and the lead aircar plunged without hesitation towards the darkest part of the shadow under the rock, just as it was programmed to do. It disappeared into the wall as if it were swallowed by the Mountain. Arenh and Mikah followed in seconds and found themselves in a totally unexpected scene.

Chapter 16—The Dreamers' lair

THE MOMENT the door to the aircar opened, Arenh knew where they were. "That's the garden chime ringing," he told Mikah. "We're in the garden outside the upper entrance! I've heard that sound all my life!"

They got out of the aircar and looked around. They were parked right in front of the watchtower at the edge of the terrace. The empty aircar was a few meters away. They shared the memory of flying straight into the north face of the Mountain near the peak. But in entering the Mountain on the north side they appeared to have actually exited the Mountain towards the east.

Arenh could see people working in the fog-shrouded gardens of the terrace in the same way he himself had often worked. In many ways, the scene was familiar. But there were differences too. Indigo buntings and red finches were nesting in the tower, strange beautiful insects were gathering nectar from the flowering plants in the garden, and above the watchtower door was an inscription: *"They shall not hurt nor destroy in all my Holy Mountain"*.

Arenh pointed at the inscription. "Look Mikah! That's never been there before."

"It's familiar, though," Mikah pondered. "Where have I seen it?"

"It's the same saying that's always been inscribed above the door to the lower entrance. My father told me when I was a child that it expressed an ideal that wasn't attainable at present. He said I must have faith that someday it would become reality."

"I think that day may have come. Look at the plain! In the field nearest the lower entrance, just to the right of where those big dogs are sleeping with the lambs, that's a lion, isn't it? Eating grass with the cattle!"

"Yeah, that's a lion all right, but those aren't big dogs, Mikah, they're wolves! We're looking at a scene from the prophecy of Isaiah! That's where the inscription we just read comes from."

"Holy Mother! This gives me the chills, Arenh. What do you think it means?"

Suddenly, as they stared in astonishment, a pocket of fog began to swirl and thicken to one side of them. The mist became so thick it appeared to be solid and transformed itself into the shape of the Ancient Mother.

"Oh crap!" Mikah whispered. "That looks just like the statue in the zendo—except she seems to have lost her sword and flower."

"That's not a statue Mikah! She looks to be as alive as we are!"

When the Ancient Mother spoke, her voice was like the soft gurgling sound of flowing water, as if thousands of voices had been blended into one.

"*Did you call me, Mikah?*" she asked.

Mikah was speechless, and Arenh was afraid he was going to faint. The Ancient Mother smiled the most beautiful and serene smile they had ever seen. Arenh and Mikah immediately relaxed as a feeling of security and well-being washed over them.

"What you see is your world as it will become and as it is already from where we watch."

"Are you one of the Dreamers?" Arenh asked.

"The Dreamers are many, and yet the many are one. We appear to you as the Ancient Mother who gave birth to your race, though your race in reality gave birth to the Ancient Mother."

"She doesn't look all that ancient to me," Mikah whispered to Arenh. Arenh looked at him in disbelief.

"The shattered petals of a rose are as beautiful as the bud, Mikah. We are all great beings, beings of light."

"Yes, but roses are different from people," Mikah replied. "And while we may all be great beings, the Dreamers have powers that people don't. Can you tell us what kind of beings the Dreamers are?"

"The Dreamers are what you are. We are all dreamers, and all these worlds are our dreams. But we who whisper in your mind are the Dreamers of the Great Dream, the Dream of the Holy Mountain."

"I don't understand," Mikah said.

"Countless Dreamers of the present age and of ages past and the Dreamers of ages to come are dreaming of a world in which all beings live in harmony and peace, and you yourselves are among us."

"We came to visit you with certain questions in mind," Arenh said, "but your answers are so large and our questions are so small. They now seem too unimportant to ask."

"*What is real is what is important, Arenh, and reality is neither large nor small. Is a grain of sand less real than a mountain? Is the ocean more real than a drop of water?*"

"Will you tell us, then, who killed Adhalmar of the Emerald Clan?"

"*The shaman who serves Orokh, the Ourdhu chief.*"

Arenh and Mikah were stunned.

"Orokh sent him?" Mikah asked.

"*Orokh has no knowledge of it. But his ignorance is less than that of the shaman, who thinks he knows when he doesn't. And the shaman's ignorance is less than that of one who thinks he doesn't know when in fact he does, which is the danger that you, Arenh, should watch for.*"

"Now I'm the one who doesn't understand," Arenh said.

"*The shaman has the power to project his dream body but has no understanding of what he does. He believes the God of the Mountain answered his prayers.*"

"I remember," Arenh said to Mikah, "that Orokh once called *me* the God of the Mountain. I think I understand now. Orokh pledged all his people to my service in return for sparing their lives. But the gods we serve in reality serve us. The shaman prayed to me to destroy Adhalmar, so his dream body assumed my image to do the deed."

"Who would have thought?" Mikah mumbled. "Though to be honest, the answer confuses me more than the question. But something that confuses me even more is how Adhalmar was able to kill your father."

Mikah looked at the Ancient Mother. "Why didn't the Dreamers warn our fathers about the plot to kill Lord Ivanh," he asked, "just as you warned Arenh and me about the demon's egg?"

"We influence the things of time through our mindlink with those who experience time. The mindlink, however, is fragile. It's like a reflection on the placid surface of a lake. The slightest wind of discord can disturb it. Let your fathers show you how it happened."

The figure of the Ancient Mother dissolved as the fog that had formed her image transformed itself into the shapes of Lord Ivanh and King Edmunh.

"Don't give him the Amulet," Edmunh pleaded. *"Please, Ivanh. Let him try to kill me. I'm sure Jonah and my guards can protect me. Please! You must not give him the Amulet!"*

Ivanh replied, *"We have talked about this enough, Edmunh. The matter is settled. Adhalmar thinks the mind powers of the Indigo Lords come from the Amulet. But he is wrong. I must give it to him. I can't bear to lose you, and I think no one can protect you from his assassins!"*

The image of Edmunh faded as an image of Adhalmar formed from the fog. Ivanh handed him the Amulet. But when Adhalmar tried to put it around his neck, it disappeared. Then the image of Adhalmar transformed itself into the image of a hooded assassin who stabbed Lord Ivanh in the heart.

Arenh gasped in shock as he saw his father fall. Mikah embraced him and forced him to turn his back on the scene. They found themselves instantly relocated to the cavern of the aerial vehicles within the Mountain. They were standing in the same hangar where they stood when they began their journey. The two aircars were resting nearby.

"End of interview. Thank you, Ancient Mother," Mikah said. "One might wonder why the personification of compassion couldn't find a more compassionate way to show someone how his father died."

"I don't think there was a painless way to answer the question," Arenh said. "And besides, I don't think the Dreamers see death the way we do."

"Why do you think that?"

"Because I think they *are* the dead. At least many of them are. I think many others may not be born yet—at least from our perspective."

"I don't understand how that could be," Mikah said. "But I think I do understand now what happened between our fathers. The plot was never to kill my father, but yours."

"But our fathers didn't see that," Arenh pointed out. "Their mindlink had been damaged by their disagreement. And yet their disagreement grew out of their concern for each other."

"I wonder..." Mikah said suspiciously. "We found ourselves standing right where we were standing before we left. Do you think we really went anywhere? Or was this all in our heads?"

"If I understood the Dreamers, Mikah, nothing exists outside of our heads—and that includes our heads! '*All these worlds are our dreams*'."

"Oh this is too deep for a simple mind like mine," Mikah said. "Do you think they were denying the reality of the external world?"

"No. I think they were denying the *externality* of the *real* world!"

"Hold that thought! I don't want it to get loose and start running around in my mind."

"Sorry," Arenh laughed.

"It's okay. You may as well let it join the pack. The one about some of the Dreamers not being born yet is top dog. I can see how dead people could still be dreaming. It's hard, but I can manage it. What I don't see is how people who aren't born yet can be doing *anything*."

"I believe," Arenh said, "that to the Dreamers, time is just a linear way of organizing the events of consciousness. I think it may be inherent in human consciousness to organize things that way. But the Dreamers may see things from many temporal perspectives. What we see as a single stream of 3D events flowing from past to future, they may perceive as a four-dimensional whole. When I received the Amulet, they whispered, '*What is past remains even now, and what is yet to come is already here*'."

"You're not really helping things at all, Arenh. The hounds are really tearing the place up in here!"

"Well, think of it this way. We've known since precolonial times that there's no absolute temporal order of events. That's just another way of saying that God doesn't have a timeline. Something we think precedes us in time may appear to come after us to someone in another part of the universe."

"I still don't see how people who aren't born yet can be doing anything," Mikah insisted.

"Maybe they're not born yet from our point of view, but from their point of view, maybe we're not born yet. But here we are. And every choice we make affects everything that's ever happened or ever will happen."

"I guess I'm not paying attention," Mikah said, "because it sounds to me like you're saying that what we do in the present not only affects the future, but the past too."

"Right."

"No, that can't be right."

"I mean yes, that's what I'm saying," Arenh chuckled. "But I don't know if it's right or not. I could argue, though, that if we accept the proposition that there's no absolute timeline for all events and if we also accept the proposition that everything is interconnected, then we're practically forced to the conclusion that what we do in the present affects the past as well as the future."

"So you really believe that what we do in the present can change the past?"

"Yes. I believe that what will happen in the future is influencing us now, and what's happening now has already influenced what happened in the past."

"You know what I think?"

"Yes," Arenh grinned. "But tell me anyway."

"I think you don't know any more than I know. You just have a knack for confusing people like me who don't know any better, like the illiterate guy who had all the illiterate people in his village believing he could read."

"You're on to me, my friend!" Arenh laughed.

Mikah looked pensive for a moment. "I just had a thought—"

120

"I was hoping that would happen soon."

"Arenh!— Stop! One smart ass in a relationship is enough, and I already have the job. Now listen. I just had a thought about the story we've heard all our lives that the first Terran colonists on Ourdh didn't know how they got here. They went to sleep in the comfort of home and family somewhere in the Solar System and woke up in the caverns of the Mountain. I had never thought before today that this story may be true! They may have all shared the same dream, and the dream became real for them."

"And don't you think the Ourdhu must have been sharing the dream too?"

"Could be," Mikah said. "I think the Ourdhu are involved in a lot more than we ever thought. I was really surprised when the Dreamers said Orokh's shaman murdered Adhalmar!"

"Yes," Arenh said thoughtfully. "We have to ask Orokh about that soon."

"Yesterday would be good."

"Or tomorrow," Arenh chuckled, amused at Mikah's attempt to escape the linear organization of consciousness. "But let's find Kodhi and Jonah now."

"Good idea."

Chapter 17—Counseling councilors

MIKAH and Arenh decided to walk from the Mountain to the City to look for Jonah and Kodhi. Arenh suggested they walk in silence as a part of their mind training for the day. The distance was hardly more than a kilometer, so they made it last as long as possible by walking slowly.

Mikah was the first to break silence. "I'm sure Jonah and Kodhi will be hanging out at the barracks of the Guard," he told Arenh when they arrived at the west gate of the Crimson Sector.

"Good! We'll get a chance to go through the gardens on our way there."

The stone path that led around the Palace to the barracks behind it was bordered on both sides with flowering trees, shrubs, and vines. They followed the path at an unhurried pace, lingering at a couple of places while they chatted. When they arrived at the barracks, they found Jonah and Kodhi there as Mikah had predicted.

"Where have you two been?" Jonah asked. "We've been trying to find you. Our operatives among the Council staff uncovered some answers to our questions about the indictment."

"But first," Kodhi said, "we need you to know something we did. You're not going to like it."

"Not to worry, my friend. There's nothing we like more than a good confession," Mikah told him.

Kodhi didn't appear convinced. "When we couldn't find you, we were afraid the Council had decided to take you out of the picture," he said anxiously, "so we told the Speaker we wanted to address the Council. We told them if we found out they had harmed either of you, we would kill them all. We had a squad of the androids with us. They got real scared—the councilors I mean, not the androids. After we left, we learned they rescinded the indictment and adjourned indefinitely."

Arenh wanted to laugh, but realized Kodhi wasn't trying to be funny. "We should have told you more about what we were doing," he said. "This is our fault, but it may not be so bad. We may be able to turn this to our advantage."

"We still don't know where you've been," Jonah said with an ambivalent tone—as if he wanted to know, but was afraid to find out.

"The Dreamers invited us to visit them," Mikah said matter-of-factly.

Kodhi and Jonah looked at each other with that should-we-call-the-psych-techs-now-or-later look.

"We'll tell you about it in a moment," Arenh grinned. "But first we need to hear your report about the Council."

"We discovered a conspiracy," Jonah said, "involving a group of merchants, a few members of the nobility, and a few of the councilors to take possession of the lands of the Ourdhu. The conspirators are mostly from the Emerald Clan, but the Speaker is one of them. They say this is our *manifest destiny*."

"We've heard that one before," Mikah observed. "But I still don't understand what they had to gain by the indictment."

"They thought the key to success in grabbing the Ourdhu lands was to get rid of you and Arenh," Jonah replied. "So they started with Arenh. I doubt they've given up. They're just regrouping. I think we need to warn Orokh."

"I wonder if we shouldn't warn the Council instead," Arenh countered.

"Warn the Council!?" Kodhi sounded as if he couldn't believe his ears.

"Let me explain," Arenh said. "The Dreamers appeared to us in the form of the Ancient Mother. She said that what the chambermaid saw was a dream body of an Ourdhu shaman. He thinks I'm a god. He saw Adhalmar as the leader of their enemies among our people, so he prayed to me to eliminate him."

"And *you* answered his prayer!" Jonah said.

"I'm sure he sees it that way," Arenh replied. "He doesn't understand that he was projecting his own consciousness in my form."

"Great Mother!" Kodhi exclaimed, suddenly seeing the light. "When he finds out that Adhalmar was only one of their enemies, he'll kill them all! Arenh's double is going to be busy. I know you'll want to stop it, Arenh, but remember," he pointed his finger as though he were lecturing, "we must not interfere with the native culture!"

They all laughed. Arenh thought how much more relaxed and playful Kodhi had become since he started working so closely with Jonah.

Mikah said, "Being the devil's advocate a moment, if what you say is true, Arenh, then why have the Ourdhu been fighting us with sticks and stones for so long? Why not kill us all with their mental projections?"

"I doubt the shaman has been able to do this in the past," Arenh answered. "It was actually seeing a god appear and disappear that empowered him."

"We may not need to warn Orokh, but I still think we need to talk to him," Jonah suggested.

"Yes. I plan to visit the chief soon," Arenh told him. "But right now I want to reconvene the Council and address the Chamber. Do you think you and Kodhi can round them up?"

Jonah looked at Kodhi wearily. "We better get on it, compadre. We'll be lucky to get all those vipers back in the nest before the end of the day."

It took a couple of hours for Kodhi and Jonah to find the Speaker and other key members of the Council and another hour to convince them it was safe for the Council to reconvene. It was late afternoon before the Council came to order and called Arenh to testify.

Arenh told them he understood their concerns, but assured them that someone had tried to frame him. He said there were witnesses who could place him in the Mountain at the time of the murder. Arenh also pointed out that he could have legally ordered Adhalmar's execution, but had decided against it. Even so, he consented to stand trial if the Council insisted.

The Speaker, however, entertained a resolution, which passed unanimously, that declared Arenh's statement sufficient. Arenh and Mikah both sensed that the Speaker was concerned that Arenh could be asked questions in the course of the trial that the Speaker didn't want asked—and, even more, didn't want answered. "He suspects that we know about the conspiracy to grab the lands of the Ourdhu," they thought together.

Chapter 18—Brothers

THE DAY following his exoneration, Arenh went to visit Orokh, accompanied only by Myra. Mikah and Kodhi had objected, not wanting to risk the two of them going without an escort. But Arenh had said they must trust Orokh if they wanted Orokh to trust them. Nevertheless, Kodhi sent two androids to accompany them. Arenh consented provided the androids would remain aboard the ship.

Myra told Arenh during the trip to the village that she and Branunh had made much progress in programming the Ourdhu language into the automated translator. She gave Arenh a headset and mouthpiece. She had brought three more units—one for herself, one for Orokh, and an extra. Each unit contained an automated translation module within the headset. The modules were capable of learning and could improve their performance as they were used.

Myra said that she had made a mistake about the gesture in which Arenh and Orokh had grasped each other's forearms while each placed a hand on the other's shoulder. She had thought it simply meant *we are brothers.* "It can mean that," she assured him. "But it also can mean *we are one* or *we are the same*—or maybe any combination of those. But all the meanings are good."

After the aircar had sat down outside the village, Myra and Arenh got out and waited. In a few minutes, they saw Orokh emerge from the village gate and walk towards them with his wife, who appeared to be pregnant.

"I think he may have misunderstood our relationship," Myra whispered.

Both Orokh and his wife were dressed in simple brown clothing. His wife had on a tunic and Orokh wore a kilt. He was shirtless as usual.

Arenh handed one of the headsets to Orokh and another to his wife. Then he and Myra put their headsets on. Orokh followed suit immediately and motioned for his wife to do so too. She was hesitant, but did as Orokh wished.

"They're harmless," Myra assured Orokh's wife. "They just help us to understand each other's language." Orokh and his wife were both startled to hear the translation in their headphones.

After exchanging greetings, Arenh said to Orokh, "Something has happened that I need to discuss with you if you have time now for us to visit."

Orokh said, "My brother and his wife are always welcome. We will go to our house to talk."

Myra said, "I'm not, uh— I'm his helper, not his wife."

Orokh's wife looked at her husband quickly, and Arenh thought that perhaps Myra had broken some taboo such as speaking directly to another woman's husband.

Myra looked at Arenh and said, "The word for *helper* can also mean *servant* or *slave*, but I thought that would be better than being your wife."

Arenh replied with a tone of feigned shock and disbelief, without thinking about Orokh and his wife being able to hear their conversation, "You would rather be my slave than my wife, Myra?"

Myra looked a little disconcerted. Orokh was clearly amused, and his wife appeared to bite her lip to keep from laughing. The ice had been broken.

"My name is Meganh," Orokh's wife said in a self-assured voice. "Please be our guests."

The walk to Orokh's house took longer than Arenh had expected because they had to greet the villagers, who had lined up on both sides of the path. "They have never seen a god before," Orokh explained.

"I'm not a god you know," Arenh replied.

"Yes, I know," Orokh said. "You are my brother. But they think you are a god. And we must not try to explain too many things at once."

"I see," Arenh said. "Then a god I will be."

"But Meganh also knows you are my brother. And I also told our mother. She always had faith that she would see you again. I was hoping she would live until you returned. But she has departed us since we last saw one another."

Arenh was stunned into silence for a moment by what Orokh had said, but at the same time he felt grief from Orokh, deep painful grief. So he pushed it all out of his consciousness and refused to think about it. He put his hand on Orokh's shoulder but said nothing. Orokh put his hand on top of Arenh's.

Myra was becoming concerned. "He thinks," she whispered to Arenh, "that you are literally his brother—his twin brother."

"She does not know?" Orokh asked with a puzzled look.

Arenh didn't want the chief to know that he was as confused as Myra, so he said, "No, my brother. Please explain to her."

Orokh then explained to Myra that it was the custom of his people that when a couple had more than two children, which would often happen when a woman gave birth to twins, a baby was sometimes given to a childless couple or to a couple who had lost their only child. This custom helped to keep families to the ideal of two children.

Many centuries earlier, Orokh told Myra, after a plague in which many babies died, the Ourdhu would steal babies from the Mountain people or the people of the plain. The Ourdhu had since abolished this practice. But when one of the Mountain dwellers who had no child had appeared to Orokh's father in a dream, his father had offered him one of the twin boys who had just been born to him and his wife. It was a way to apologize for the wrongs the Ourdhu had committed in years past, and Orokh's father hoped it might end the war.

As Orokh talked, Arenh realized that his father, Lord Ivanh, was the Mountain dweller to whom Orokh's father had given a child. His mother, Lady Julia, was not his birth mother. Orokh was indeed his twin brother. And he, Arenh, was Ourdhu! He suddenly felt the urge to leave. He wanted to return to the Mountain quickly. He wanted to talk to his mother and to Mikah. It took all the discipline he could muster to suppress his urge to run. He had to remember the reason they had come to see Orokh.

Orokh noticed his agitation. "Are you feeling sick?" he asked in a concerned voice.

"Oh, no," Arenh said. "I'll be fine. Let's find a place to sit and talk."

Orokh and Meganh led them into their house and offered chairs. They all sat down around a table while Meganh left to get a pitcher of water.

Arenh sat in silence. He felt as though he no longer knew who he was. Everything he assumed about himself was suddenly called into question. Orokh seemed to accept his silence as natural.

When Meganh returned, she poured a cup of water for Arenh and then sat down beside Orokh.

Arenh drank it all. "Thank you," he told Meganh.

"I'm sorry. I thought you understood," Orokh said quietly through the translator. "I can see it must have been a shock for a prince of the Mountain to find out his twin is Ourdhu."

Arenh looked at Orokh with a new appreciation. He felt a deep affection for him, as though he had known him all his life. "I should have known I couldn't deceive you, Orokh. You are after all my brother. And I've never met anyone who could deceive *me* for long, though I've developed a troubling capacity to deceive myself."

"No one else needs to know," Orokh said.

Arenh had been so preoccupied with his identity crisis that he had failed to see its effect on his brother. "I'm proud you're my brother, Orokh. Please don't misunderstand my surprise."

"My people will regard me more highly for having a brother who is the God of the Mountain. But your people will not think so highly of you if they discover you are Ourdhu."

"Your people and mine need to see the truth," Arenh replied, "that we are all brothers and sisters."

"Yes, and we must help them to see that when the time is right," Orokh agreed. "But not now. Now I think we should talk about why you came to visit. You said something has happened that you needed to discuss."

"Yes," Arenh agreed. "Something very disturbing has happened." He told the story of the murder of Adhalmar and how he had been accused of the killing. He didn't mention the Dreamers, but said that he believed only a powerful shaman could have been the real murderer.

Orokh was concerned. He apologized. He said the village shaman had overheard in a dream of a plot to steal the lands of the Ourdhu. The shaman had seen Arenh on his previous visit to the village and was impressed at Arenh's ability to appear and disappear. He had told Orokh that he would pray to the God of the Mountain to destroy the leader of the thieves.

"The shaman has much knowledge," Orokh said, "but little wisdom. And I had no idea his prayers could cause someone to die!"

"Do you think he understands that the gods and demons he conjures up are creations of his own mind?"

"I'm sure he doesn't. I'm only beginning myself to understand the power of the mind, since I met you."

"Maybe the shaman needs your guidance, my brother," Arenh suggested.

"Meganh and I will talk to him together," Orokh agreed. "He listens to me, but he trusts her more. He is her father's brother, and she is like a daughter to him since he has no children."

"Thank you for your kindness," Arenh said. "If the thieves among the people of the plain threaten your borders, the people of the Mountain will join you to stop them. You have my word as your brother. But I don't think they will be so foolish. We must go now. We will return soon. We will have much to talk about when I return, so please keep the translation devices." Arenh leaned forward and kissed Orokh on the forehead and then did the same to Meganh.

Meganh took Arenh's hand in hers for a moment as a way of saying goodbye. Orokh walked back with Arenh and Myra to the waiting aircar. Again the villagers lined the path on both sides. But this time Arenh, Myra, and Orokh walked straight to the aircar without pausing to talk to them.

Arenh was grateful that the car could find its own way back. After Myra and he were safely aboard and on their way home, Myra said, "Would you like to tell me what just happened now or later, My Lord?"

"Later, Myra. Please. I'm sorry, but I need time to understand it myself."

Myra nodded her acceptance of this. "Please let me know if I can help."

"Please wait a few days before you tell anyone what Orokh said about us being brothers. Don't even tell Branunh. Not until I let Mikah know. I don't want Mikah to hear this from anyone else."

"As you wish, sir," Myra replied calmly. But inside she was excited. "For years we've been wondering how to bridge the chasm between us and the Ourdhu," she thought, "and the solution has been in our midst all that time!" She was shocked when Arenh responded to her thought.

"I see the possibility too, Myra, of using my origins as a bridge to unite humankind on our planet. But I can't let myself think about that yet. Remember that legally the Ourdhu aren't considered human by the High Council. That's another reason you must tell no one right now."

"I wonder if he can read minds?" she thought.

Arenh looked at her and smiled but said nothing.

"Are you human?" she asked.

"Yes, of course. The Ourdhu are human."

"Forgive me, sir, for asking such a thing. It's just that you seem superhuman in some ways. But I've seen the DNA studies. The law declaring that the Ourdhu aren't human is absurd. You may as well declare that the Western Sea isn't water."

"Yes," Arenh laughed. "That nonsense has been on the books for centuries, and we have to fix it soon."

Chapter 19—A mother's love

ARENH took Myra back to the City and then ordered the aircar to take him home. He went straight to his mother's apartment. Donna answered the door. She seemed a bit cool. Perhaps because he hadn't called ahead for her to expect him? Or maybe she was just worried about something. He had never felt the slightest negative feeling from her before.

"I'm sorry for not calling ahead, Donna. But I was so lost in my thoughts I forgot, and I need to see Mother as soon as possible."

"You know your mother will always see you, Arenh." He felt her feelings soften. "Let me tell her you're here."

In a few moments, she came back and said, "She's waiting for you, dear. And Arenh, be kind to her, please."

He wondered why she would say that.

"What a pleasant surprise to see you," his mother said as he walked in. "But I think whatever brings you to see me so unexpectedly is most likely not pleasant. Is Mikah all right?"

"Yes, I think so," Arenh said. "I haven't seen him today, but I would know if something were wrong."

"Yes, I understand," she said. Arenh thought she probably did.

"I visited Orokh, the Ourdhu chief today." He felt his mother's mind tighten with anxiety when he mentioned Orokh. On the outside, she was as calm as ever. But inside he could feel the turmoil rising.

"It's okay," he told her. "I know. I just wondered why you and father didn't tell me."

"We never planned to keep anything from you. You were my very own dear little baby, and I couldn't have loved you more if I had given birth to you myself."

"You were infertile?"

"Yes. Your father could have divorced me and taken another wife, but he would never do that."

"How did Father meet the Ourdhu chief who was my birth father?"

"I was never clear about that. He said they met in a dream. But that makes no sense at all to me."

"The Ourdhu chief I met today is my twin."

"Oh my! No wonder you were upset. Are you identical?"

"I'm not sure. It's hard to tell. He wears a full beard and keeps his hair at shoulder length."

"I'm sorry, for what that's worth."

He leaned over and kissed her forehead. "You have nothing to be sorry for. I like my brother very much. And I've never doubted your love. Or Father's. You're my mother, just like you've always been and always will be."

She got up from her chair, something she seldom did when receiving a guest, and extended her arms for Arenh to hug her. Arenh embraced her and held her close.

"Thank you. This should have happened years ago," she said. "But that ridiculous law. I was afraid."

"Will you tell Donna why I was so rude as to appear without calling first?"

"Of course. But she already understands I'm sure. She's known about this for years. And ever since you brought the Ourdhu chief back to his home, we've both known it was just a matter of time and you would know."

"It's strange, isn't it," Arenh said, "how we worry about such trivial things?"

"I know it's not trivial. You're just trying to make me feel better. That's very sweet." She hesitated a moment and then asked, "You haven't talked to Mikah yet about this have you?"

"No, I wanted to talk to you first."

"You must go and talk to Mikah."

"I'm afraid to. I'm sure Mikah will say all the right words. He always does. What I'm afraid of is what he really feels. I know he risks his position to protect the native people, but that doesn't mean he wants to be sleeping with one."

He realized he had said too much. There were very few things going on around his mother that she didn't know about. There were a lot of things, though, that she preferred not to talk about.

But his mother seemed undisturbed. "If he doesn't love you anymore because of this, Arenh, then he never really loved you. You must go and talk to him."

Chapter 20—The alien lover

AFTER leaving his mother's apartment, Arenh used the Amulet to relocate outside Mikah's office. He knocked on the door.

"You know you don't have to knock Arenh," Mikah called out.

Mikah was busy reading proposed legislation. "You can help if you wish," he told Arenh. "I don't have anyone yet that I trust to help me sort out what's important from what's trivial."

"You could ask Jonah or Kodhi or Leah."

"They have too much to do already."

"I'd be glad to help, but you know my opinion may be different from yours." The remark was sincere. Arenh was happy to have any activity on which to concentrate his attention and prevent Mikah from knowing his thoughts.

"We may have different opinions about something important, but we're likely to be in agreement about what's trivial," Mikah said. "Here, you take this stack."

They worked an hour or more until at least one of them had reviewed every document on the table.

"And this is only for two days," Mikah said. "Most of it's nonsense. They get into things they have no business in."

"Like declaring the Ourdhu to be nonhuman," Arenh said.

"Yes. That's the crowning absurdity, and it's been on the books for centuries. I've had one of my allies in the Council introduce a measure to repeal that law and another to issue an apology to the Ourdhu—not that they will ever know."

"One of them will know."

"What was that?"

"I said one of the Ourdhu will know."

"Yes, of course, you mean your friend Orokh. But my guess is he probably doesn't know about the original law."

"Not Orokh." Arenh released his mental blocks and let his thoughts and feelings flow freely for Mikah to share.

As Mikah began to feel the flood of images and feelings from Arenh's mind, he got up from the table where they had been working and motioned for Arenh to follow him to a sofa.

"I'm not used to you hiding things from me," he said. He was clearly hurt.

"I was afraid of what you would think."

"Now that really hurts—that you would be afraid of me."

"It's not every day a guy discovers he's been sleeping with an alien."

"If he's a beautiful, kind-hearted, super-intelligent alien, what would it matter? Now your thoughts were clear on the essentials, but I'm a little fuzzy on a couple of details. So why don't you tell me the whole story."

Arenh relaxed. "Hug first," he said.

Mikah held him tight for a few moments and then said, "Okay. Now I want to hear it all, from the beginning."

"I think this is a great opportunity," Mikah said when Arenh had finished his story. "I bet you aren't the first Ourdhu child to be raised as one of our people. And from what Orokh said, many Terran children must have been raised as Ourdhu centuries ago, when they still practiced abduction. Even without the genetic intermingling, we have no scientific basis for considering Terrans and Ourdhu to be different, except culturally. And now it's clear many of us are kin."

"I thought of that," Arenh said,

"Yeah, that's probably what made *me* think of it," Mikah laughed.

"You know I didn't mean it that way. I was thinking that since I have no children—and don't plan to have any—I need to name an heir. There's no reason for me not to name one of my nephews or nieces as my heir."

"Can you name a niece as heir under Indigo law?"

"Not now, but I plan to change that. I noticed Meganh is pregnant, probably a little further along than Leah. So when you have a son, I may already have a newborn nephew or niece."

"But wouldn't you need to raise the child? That's the custom, isn't it? Meganh isn't likely to take kindly to parting with her baby."

"Yeah, I thought of— God! I have to stop saying that. Yes, you're right. I know it's a crazy idea. But Orokh and Meganh already have a son and a daughter. The Ourdhu don't usually have more than that. I doubt this pregnancy was planned. That doesn't mean they would love the baby any less, but the sharing of infants under those circumstances with someone who is childless is a well-established and honored custom among the valley people."

"Uncle Arenh," Mikah mumbled. "Has a nice ring. My son will call you uncle too."

"Wouldn't it be nice if you and Leah would have a daughter next. And if I adopt my nephew, your daughter and he could marry and—"

"Wait, wait!" Mikah stopped him. "Too many *ifs*. Life is like a chess game. It's a waste of time to plan too many moves ahead. So why don't we just lock the door and lie here on the sofa awhile and relax."

"Relax?"

"Yeah, I find making love very relaxing," Mikah grinned. "Especially with an alien."

Chapter 21—Princess Maria

ARENH had promised Orokh another visit soon. He decided to visit alone this time. Kodhi wanted to send a guard with him, but Arenh refused. Kodhi insisted, as he had on Arenh's last visit to the Ourdhu, and they compromised again on a couple of androids who would remain on the ship. Arenh made sure he had the headset with him that Myra had provided on their last trip to see Orokh.

Orokh seemed to be expecting Arenh when he arrived. Arenh was shocked when he saw him. Orokh had shaved and cut his hair in the same style as Arenh. There was no doubt they were identical twins. Orokh was able to know Arenh's thoughts occasionally, and Arenh could often feel Orokh's thoughts and emotions. Arenh realized there must be a strong psychic connection between the two of them that was growing stronger, though he didn't share the flow of Orokh's mental events in the way he did Mikah's.

Arenh didn't mention the idea he had shared with Mikah about adopting Orokh's child. But he didn't need to. Orokh took him into the bedroom to see Meganh. She was lying in bed with a baby on each breast.

"Twins," Orokh said.

Arenh noticed that he didn't use the translator.

"You have no children, Arenh?"

Arenh shook his head no.

Orokh bent over and kissed one of the infants and said, "This one is your son, my brother."

Meganh nodded her agreement, but Arenh could feel the sadness in her.

"It has to be," she said through her translator. "And with you, he's still in our family. You are his father's brother. I will get to see him often, and he will be a prince of the Mountain dwellers."

"Is the other one also a boy?" Arenh asked.

"A little girl," Meganh said.

"I'll be as happy with a daughter as with a son," Arenh told them.

Orokh said they had assumed he would want the little boy so he would have an heir. Meganh had preferred to keep the boy because the Ourdhu chief had to be a male. Arenh explained that he had issued a decree that permitted either a male or female to inherit the Indigo Cloak.

"Of course," he told Orokh, "a woman doesn't usually wear a chlamys unless she's a military officer. But if I can change the law, she can change the fashion. I'm sure she can wear a lovely floor-length chiton under it and set a new trend."

"What will her name be?" Orokh asked.

Arenh had considered this question before his visit—in the event Meganh gave birth to a girl. He would use the "M" from Mikah, the "Ar" from his own name, and the "ia" from his mother's name—Princess Maria.

"Someday," Arenh told them, "she will be Princess Maria, Lord of the Indigo Clan."

Meganh repeated the name and title with great pride. "I can visit?" she asked.

"You and Orokh will have your own apartment in the Mountain if you wish and an aircar to travel back and forth from the village."

Orokh and Arenh talked for a long time and discussed many things, sometimes using the translator and sometimes not. When it came time for Arenh to leave, Meganh wanted him to take the baby with him right away. She said the longer she nursed the child, the stronger their bond would be and the more painful it would be to part. Arenh agreed and said he would return the next morning with a nurse.

When Arenh left Orokh's village, he decided to visit Mikah and Leah before returning to the Mountain to tell his mother of his new niece and adopted daughter. He found Mikah in his office.

"You remember we talked about the possibility of me naming one of my nephews as my heir?" Arenh asked.

"Meganh had her baby?" Mikah asked in reply.

"Yes," Arenh informed him. "Both of them."

"She had twins."

"Yes. I've named the one I'm adopting Maria."

"You named him Maria?" Mikah asked with an incredulous tone.

"I named *her* Maria," Arenh chuckled. "She's very beautiful. I haven't had a chance to get acquainted with her yet. Meganh wants me to take her right away. Of course, she's not weaned yet. So I have to find a nurse."

"Let's talk to Leah," Mikah said. "Our child is due very soon. I don't know how she will feel about nursing two babies."

The two of them walked together to Leah's apartment. As soon as Arenh told her of his adopted daughter, she asked if he had a nurse for the child.

Arenh replied, "Not yet."

"I'm lactating already," Leah said. "Let me go with you tomorrow. What will you name her?"

"Maria," Arenh told her.

"Very nice," she said. "Is it a name of a grandmother or aunt?"

Arenh told her how he arrived at the name.

"Mikah," she said, "do you think we could combine the names of your father and Arenh's in a similar way for our son?"

Mikah thought a moment. "*Idmunh* doesn't work," he replied. "Maybe *Evanh*?"

Arenh and Leah had to laugh.

"*Evanh* is a real possibility," she said. "Is it settled then?" She looked at Arenh. "I'll be Maria's nurse?"

"If it's okay with Mikah."

"It was my idea," Mikah said. "I would like to go with you and meet Orokh and his wife."

"We'll see if Jonah and Kodhi will allow us to go with only a couple of androids and a warbot or two," Arenh said. "My guess is that with all three of us— almost four of us—going, they'll want to send a fleet of warbots and a carrier full of troops."

Arenh was right. The next day a small fleet of warbots and troop carriers landed in front of the Ourdhu village. Orokh and Meganh met them outside the gate while the villagers watched from inside. Meganh held her baby girl in her arms. She had left the other infant with a nurse so that she and Orokh could accompany Arenh, Mikah, and Leah to the Mountain with the newly named Princess Maria.

When they arrived at the Mountain, Lady Julia was waiting for them with Donna. Arenh had never seen his mother so happy.

While introductions were being made, Mikah motioned Arenh aside and said, "Your brother's a knockout."

"Since he looks exactly like me," Arenh replied, "I suppose I should say thank you."

"He seems to feel at home in the Mountain," Mikah observed.

"I think the Mountain may be his ancestral home."

"What makes you think that?"

"My DNA matched that of the dead cells in the original AI module."

"That's mind-boggling!" Mikah replied. "You think the Ourdhu were the builders of the Mountain?"

"Not the Ourdhu as we know them today," Arenh said, "but their ancestors. I believe they came here from some other world, and the Mountain was probably a captured asteroid they used for their ship. They must have left their progeny on many planets, which is why you and I are both human. I

146

think Ourdh was the end of their journey, though I'm sure we still hear their voices in the whispers of the Dreamers."

While Mikah was trying to wrap his mind around what Arenh had said, Orokh walked over to join them.

"My brothers!" Orokh greeted them with his right fist against his abdomen.

Arenh returned the gesture. "Mikah was just saying that you seem to feel right at home here."

"Two members of my family live here," Orokh replied with a smile. "I feel I'm among friends."

Arenh put one hand on Mikah's shoulder and the other on Orokh's. "You *are* among friends," he told Orokh. "And I would like for the Mountain to be your home too. I promised you and Meganh an apartment here. I hope you will accept."

"Of course, my brother. We are very grateful."

After making small talk awhile, Orokh took his leave. Arenh made him a gift of an aircar, a pair of server bots, and a squad of androids.

"I want to be sure you can travel safely between your home in the village and your new home in the Mountain," he explained.

Arenh also convinced Leah and Mikah to take an apartment in the Mountain as a second home, at least until their baby arrived. That would make them closer to the medical facility in the Mountain when the time came. He was also thinking of his mother, who he knew wanted to be near her new granddaughter.

Chapter 22—A date with doom

LEAH and Mikah accepted Arenh's offer of the apartment in the Mountain, though it was small and simply-furnished compared to what they were accustomed to in the Palace. A few days later they realized how fortunate this decision had been. Two Emerald assassins infiltrated the Crimson Palace at night and broke into Leah's bedchamber. They died there at the hands of Jonah's guardsmen. But if the Queen and her unborn child had been there with Maria, they would have died also.

Mikah was in the Palace at the time, but Jonah and Kodhi transported him to the Mountain in case the attack was part of a larger plan. They went to Arenh's apartment as soon as they arrived.

"It looks as if you were wrong about Karl," Jonah told Arenh. "He must have ordered this."

"No," Arenh said. "Karl would never order the murder of an infant. But I'm afraid his mother wouldn't hesitate to murder anyone she believes stands in her way. I think I underestimated her."

"I don't understand how Emerald agents could penetrate your security," Kodhi told Jonah.

"I hold myself responsible," Jonah replied. "One of their undercover agents seduced one of our guardsmen into an affair."

Arenh noticed Jonah appeared a little uncomfortable and seemed to avoid looking at Mikah. Mikah picked up on Arenh's thoughts immediately.

"Oh no," Mikah interrupted. "Not Alinh again."

"You know him?" Kodhi asked.

Jonah answered before Mikah could say anything. "He was formerly one of Mikah's guards at the Palace, but I had to reassign him because of failure to remain at his duty post."

"Why such a lenient penalty?" Kodhi asked. "Desertion of duty station was a capital offense in the old days."

"I intervened and persuaded Jonah not to discharge him," Mikah told Kodhi. "This is all my fault."

Kodhi's eyes caught Arenh's for just a moment, and a knowing look came over his face. "I see," he said.

"No one could have foreseen how events would unfold," Arenh told Mikah, putting his hand on Mikah's shoulder in a comforting way.

"I still don't understand," Kodhi said. "And please don't take this the wrong way. I just need to learn from the mistakes of others as well as my own. And I don't see how the agent could use an affair with the guard to get in the Palace. I mean the guard didn't have access anymore, did he?"

"All the agent wanted from Alinh was access to the barracks of the Guard," Jonah replied. "Alinh shared a bunkroom with the guards assigned to Leah. After Alinh and the Emerald agent had their fun—or perhaps before—the agent tied him up and gagged him. She then let another agent in through a window. They hid there until Alinh's bunkmates returned. The Emerald agents strangled them to death, took their access badges, and entered the Palace dressed in Crimson colors.

"They knew the guards they were supposed to relieve would be suspicious. So they shot them on sight. But Alinh meanwhile had managed to struggle free and sound the alarm. The Emerald agents kicked in the door to the Queen's chamber only to find it empty. A rapid response squad arrived before they could get away. They never expected to get out alive, of course."

"Their only mistake was not to strangle Alinh," Kodhi observed in a rather analytical tone.

"My thought exactly," Arenh said.

Mikah shot him a wounded look.

"I didn't mean that like it sounded, my love," Arenh said apologetically. "What I meant was that Alinh seduced them as much as they seduced him. He has that kind of power over people."

"I wonder if Leah has heard of the attack?" Mikah asked—clearly needing to change the subject.

"I'm sure she has," Arenh replied. "Everyone in the Mountain is talking about it. We best go see her soon."

"Tell her I send my love," Jonah said sadly. "I need to get back to the Palace now and deal with the pain of losing four of our best."

"I'll tag along if you don't mind," Kodhi said.

150

After the captains had left, Arenh and Mikah talked for a while trying to make sense of the attack. Then they walked to Leah's quarters. Even though daybreak was still hours away, she and the baby were awake because of all the excitement—and because Maria was hungry. Leah had just started nursing her when the two men arrived, so they waited patiently while the little princess took her time.

"There," Leah said when Maria was done. "She'll want to go back to sleep now."

Leah handed her to Arenh, who rocked her gently until she dozed off.

"Sweet dreams, my darling," Arenh said softly as he kissed Maria on the forehead and laid her in her crib.

"We were afraid you would be worried about the reports of the attack," Mikah said as soon as Arenh rejoined them.

"Why," Leah asked, "would anyone want to kill *me*?"

"Mikah and I have been trying to make sense of it too," Arenh told her. "We think Maria was the primary target. We believe Emerald intelligence agents thought you had given birth to a son. Katrina thought she had no chance of making her own son king if Mikah had an heir. You can guess the rest."

In fact, not even Arenh could have guessed the rest. His heart was much too pure to conceive of what Katrina was capable of doing—at least until Jonah and Kodhi returned unexpectedly a while later.

"We just got back from the Emerald Palace. It looks like a battle field," Jonah reported.

"It *was* a battle field!" Kodhi said excitedly. "Lady Katrina has fled the City. Count Hugho is dead and possibly Lord Karl too. The surviving staff led us to an antimatter bomb Katrina left behind. We think the device has the capacity to destroy the whole City and maybe the Mountain too."

"When Adhalmar called her a whore he didn't miscall her by much," Jonah added. "We learned that she and Hugho have been involved romantically for some time. Since Adhalmar's death, they've been using a small force of fanatical troops to challenge Karl's authority."

"What about the weapon?" Mikah asked hopefully. "Can it be disarmed?"

"We have the best technicians from every clan working on it," Jonah replied. "But if they fail, the timer on the device indicates detonation will occur a little more than an hour from now. We've begun evacuation of as many as possible in the time we have."

"Several of the Emerald Palace staff have confided in us," Kodhi reported. "They have surveillance cameras all over the Palace that record everything. We saw a few minutes of video in which Karl was really pissed off when he learned of the attempted assassination of Leah and Maria.

"He told Katrina 'Confine yourself to your quarters Mother!' Then he turned to Hugho. 'You sir are relieved of all command. You will be held for court martial on charges of high treason.'

"At that point, Katrina went ballistic. She screamed 'You wimp! You're no son of mine.' She told Hugho 'If you have any balls, you'll kill him right now!'

"Hugho went for his weapon, and that's when the battle began."

The story seemed to shake Mikah. "Did Karl's personal guards stand by him?" he asked.

"Most of them died defending him," Jonah replied. "But not before they took out Hugho and his key lieutenants. We believe that when Hugho fell, Katrina sent two of her troops to arm the bomb. She and her remaining guards left in a troop carrier immediately."

"The forces loyal to Karl were outnumbered in the beginning," Kodhi said. "But after two of Hugho's sub-commanders and their troops switched sides, the odds were more even. Then as news of the bomb spread, most of the troops loyal to Hugho deserted. We don't know at what point Karl fell. That wasn't on the short video we saw. But we heard his forces fought their way to a deep space cruiser near the barracks on the east side of the Palace. They carried Karl's unconscious body into the ship and left."

"We don't really know if Karl survived or not," Jonah explained. "Some survivors say he was dead. Others say he was only wounded."

"I have no doubt he was still alive when they carried him into the ship," Kodhi said. "People don't risk their lives like that for a corpse."

"And what about Katrina?" Arenh asked Kodhi.

"The ranking survivor of Karl's forces told us her troop carrier left on a course towards the northern lowlands. Orokh told us later that his scouts had discovered an Emerald bunker in the lowlands last year. I immediately sent a fleet of warbots to find it. When we arrived, the carrier was already there parked on top of the bunker. I saw it as clearly through the neural link as I would if I had been physically present."

"And when you left?" Arenh inquired.

"Smoke, ashes, and a big hole in the ground." Kodhi looked down to avoid Arenh's eyes. "I suppose I should have checked with you first," he said apologetically.

"No. That was your call, my friend," Arenh reassured him. "I just don't want you to think you need to hide anything from me."

"As though that were possible," Kodhi thought as he looked up at Arenh.

"I often wish it were possible," Arenh said softly.

Kodhi seemed a bit unnerved.

Mikah looked at him and smiled. "You get used to it," he said.

"I think we should go now to where the weapon is," Arenh suggested.

"No, My Lord," Kodhi protested. His tone was emphatic, but at the same time soft and affectionate. "I'm sure Jonah will agree that you and Mikah must evacuate with our families. Orokh is welcoming our people to his villages as fast as we can get them there. The shuttles are already leaving from every part of the City."

Lady Julia entered with Donna. "Come," she motioned to Leah. "Get Maria. You will leave with us, my dear." No one would instruct the Queen so directly in ordinary circumstances, but in the emergency they were suffering, Lady Julia was clearly in charge of getting civilians in the Mountain to safety.

"Arenh?" his mother said, with a worried tone.

Arenh walked over to her and kissed her. "I love you. Please don't worry. You didn't forget Achilles, did you?"

"No, my dear. No one forgets Achilles. He's very excited to be going somewhere. Promise me you'll be careful. And Arenh, please don't try to— to be a hero."

Arenh could see the tears forming in her eyes, so he hugged her tightly. "I'll be careful. I've never been the hero type," he assured her.

After the women had left, Arenh insisted on going to the location of the bomb. The four men took an aircar together towards the Emerald Palace. The airspace above the City and over the plain was swarming with aircraft.

"Looks like they've commandeered everything that could get off the ground," Kodhi observed.

Their aircar landed in front of the Emerald Palace, and Jonah and Kodhi led the way around the west side of the building to the formal garden behind it. "You don't want to see what's inside," Kodhi explained.

The device was sitting on a waist-high pedestal near the back of the garden. They had disguised it as a decorative globe. The pedestal was standing in the center of an octagonal gazebo.

The techs had removed the cover on one side of the device, and a number of them were working on it. Two of them wore Emerald colors. Several Indigo and Crimson guardsmen were there including the first officers of Jonah and Kodhi. The first officers motioned for the captains to join them. Meanwhile, one of the Indigo technicians walked over to where Arenh and Mikah were standing.

"Your Majesty, My Lord," the tech said, bowing first to Mikah and then to Arenh, "it doesn't look good. We're not sure of how much time we have left. The timer has stopped several times and then resumed. We have no idea why. We're certain the device will detonate if we stop the timer. But it sometimes stops itself. If it continues as it is now, the containment fields will collapse and annihilation will occur in just over an hour."

Arenh and Mikah watched the technicians and waited hopefully. And while they waited, they talked.

Chapter 23—A new star in the sky

I WANTED to watch my son grow up," Mikah said. "And I wanted to grow old with you and Leah."

"I myself was looking forward to being *young* with you and Leah for a while yet," Arenh smiled. "But I wanted to grow old with you, too, and to watch little Maria grow up. I would have enjoyed being a part of her life. And I would have loved to see my mother come alive again because of Maria. I can see it happening already.

"I'm grateful though that my brother will be here for them. He looks like me, and I believe he thinks and feels as I do about many things. And I hope I'll still be here in some way, too, in some way we can't understand right now. We must have faith that death isn't the end."

"Maybe so," Mikah said. "But I'm not really interested in surviving as some kind of spirit. I'm such a flesh and blood kind of guy. I want to see and hear and touch. I want to taste the salt on your skin and smell your sweat."

Arenh put his arm around Mikah's shoulder. "Have you ever dreamed of making love?"

Mikah nodded yes. "With you," he said.

"Was it good?"

Mikah nodded yes again.

"What makes things real is that we experience them together. The whole universe, I believe, is just the embodiment of our collective consciousness. It's like a huge shared dream. And when our bodies die, our dreams go on. Death is just part of the dream. So what does a flesh and blood kind of guy like you have to worry about?"

Mikah looked a little confused. "What about you?" he asked.

"Me?"

"Yeah. Have you ever dreamed of making love?"

"No. But I did dream I was in bed with you once when I farted. It was really embarrassing. You asked me to leave, which made it even worse. Does that count for a flesh and blood type dream?"

"No. That doesn't count."

"Why not?"

"Because that wasn't a dream," Mikah laughed as a tear rolled down his face. "I remember when it happened."

"How could you forget, huh? But the fact is I remember it as a dream. Are you sure it wasn't?"

"I wouldn't have been sure, except that I remember it, too."

"Right," Arenh smiled. "That's what I mean. What makes it real is that both of us experienced it. I think everything that happens is like that. It's like a big dream that all conscious beings are dreaming together—even the animals and insects."

"I just wish I were as sure as you are."

"I'm not sure of anything, my love," Arenh said softly. He took a deep breath and exhaled slowly as though he relished every molecule of air and every moment of life. "On second thought," he said, "maybe I *am* sure of one thing. If I'm standing on the brink of the abyss, and I have the choice of plunging into the unknown with hope or without hope, I'll go with hope every time."

As they talked, they glanced now and then at the timer the technicians had set up. They watched as the time they had left to live diminished from 50 minutes to 40 to 30 to 25.

Jonah and Kodhi—who had been in their own little huddle to the side after ordering their guardsmen to leave—joined Mikah and Arenh when the countdown reached 20 minutes. "Our families are safe for the time being with Orokh and Meganh," Jonah reported. "And our first officers have both sworn loyalty to Leah and Lady Julia as regents until your kids are old enough to take over."

"No! Both of you must leave," Mikah ordered.

"Kodhi and I have decided to join you two here for the end," Jonah said firmly. "You can charge us with insubordination after we're dead."

Kodhi smiled in grim appreciation of Jonah's attempt at gallows humor. "I know I owe it to my family to survive if I can," he said. "But I couldn't live with myself if I left the two of you here to die."

Arenh looked Kodhi straight in the eye and said matter-of-factly, "I'll make sure you live to die of something else, my friend." Kodhi understood. And so did Jonah. But Mikah did not.

"I'm not blocking him," Arenh thought, "so he must be blocking himself from my thoughts—he doesn't want to face what has to be."

159

Mikah appeared to be in deep concentration. "I wonder if it would be possible to load the whole thing into an aircar and take it some other place?" he asked.

"I think if it were that simple, the techs would have already done it," Jonah replied. "But it wouldn't hurt to ask."

Jonah summoned one of the technicians and asked him the question. "It has a location-sensitive switch," the tech told them. "The countdown will abort and it will detonate if we try to move it."

"If its location were to change, how long would we have before detonation?" Arenh asked.

"Not long enough," the tech said. "No more than a second or two."

After the tech had returned to his work, Arenh looked at Kodhi and Jonah. "A second or two should be more than enough," he said.

Mikah suddenly understood. "No, Arenh, you can't do that. No! Please!"

Arenh kissed him. "I love you," he whispered. And to Jonah and Kodhi he said, "Hold him."

Jonah seized one of Mikah's arms and Kodhi the other as Mikah struggled and shouted, "No! No!"

Arenh dropped his cloak and walked swiftly to the pedestal. He ordered the technicians to stand back. They appeared startled and confused but immediately complied.

"Quickly!" shouted Kodhi while Mikah fought and yelled for them to let him go.

Arenh bent over the weapon and wrapped his arms around it. He forced the Amulet on his chest

160

tight against the device and disappeared with it in his arms.

A new star suddenly appeared above the eastern horizon of the predawn sky. It flared quickly to outshine the brightest stars in the heavens, and then faded just as quickly back into the night.

Mikah struggled free of Jonah and Kodhi and ran to the spot where Arenh had stood. He fell to his knees in agony. A few of the technicians milled about asking each other questions and trying to understand what had happened, and others just gazed at the sky in awe. Jonah and Kodhi rushed to Mikah. Jonah knelt beside him and held him in his arms and whispered words of comfort to him as he wept.

Chapter 24—The Crimson heir

JONAH and Kodhi couldn't convince Mikah to leave the garden of the Emerald Palace. They reminded him of his responsibilities to the people of the clans, to Leah, and to his unborn son. They reminded him that he was now the regent for Arenh's daughter, the new Lord of the Indigo Clan. But he seemed to cling to the last place he had seen Arenh, as though he were unable to continue life without him.

Kodhi soon received a message, however, that Leah was returning from Orokh's village to the Mountain immediately. She had gone into labor during the evacuation. The news snapped Mikah back from the paralysis of his grief. An aircar sat down near them and opened its door. They entered, and a few minutes later the aircar flew into one of the open hangar bays on the western face of the Mountain. From there, they walked quickly to the medical facility.

The three men waited outside the delivery room until Wahlis, the chief medic, emerged. "You have a fine healthy little boy, Your Majesty. The Queen would like to see you now."

"What has she been told about the emergency?" Mikah asked.

"She knows what we all know, that somehow we have been spared."

Mikah had hoped Leah knew about Arenh. But he realized now that very few people knew. He looked to Jonah and Kodhi for support and then entered Leah's room.

Leah had her newborn on her breast. Maria was asleep in a nearby baby bed. "I can only nurse one of them at a time," Leah explained. "Maria is very calm and takes her time, but Mikah Jr. is a little pig," she laughed. "Do you still want to call him Evanh? I'm sure Arenh will love that. It's so similar to his father's name."

"Arenh is dead." The tears welled up in Mikah's eyes again as he feared they would. Leah was shocked into silence for a few seconds.

"I'm so sorry, Mikah," she said as her eyes also moistened with tears. "I loved Arenh, too, but I can hardly imagine your loss. How?"

"He relocated himself and the bomb. In deep space. Jonah and Kodhi held me back, and I couldn't get to him in time."

"You were going to stop him?"

"No. Who can stop Arenh? I was going to go with him."

"I guess it's selfish of me, but I'm glad they didn't let you do it, even though I know you must feel like a part of you is gone."

"Yes. We shared so much. We would feel each other's feelings and think each other's thoughts. We had much different feelings and thoughts about many things. But we shared them with each other. It was strange and wonderful. And now I feel so alone inside. I can't help but feel angry with him for leaving me. I know it's not rational. He did the only thing that could be done, the thing that had to be done. I keep reminding myself—'*Greater love has no one than this, to lay down his life for his friends*'."

"But there *is* a love that's just as great as *dying* for your friends," Leah said. "You can also love them enough to *live* for them. You aren't alone, my dear. You're surrounded by people who love you and need you. Your son needs you, Arenh's mother and daughter need you. Jonah and Kodhi and the people of the clans, Orokh and Meganh and the people of the villages—they all need you. Perhaps more than all of them, I need you." She wiped a tear from her face. "But I know you can't see it now," she continued. "Healing will take a lot of time."

Mikah remembered Arenh's misquote of the line from Dickinson. "*They say that time assuages—but time never did assuage.*" But to Leah, he smiled, as he sniffed and wiped his eyes, and said softly, "Yes, it will take a lot of time." He leaned over and kissed Leah. And then he kissed his son. He sat down on the edge of the bed and grew quiet as he watched Leah nurse their baby.

"May I hold him?" he asked when the baby was done. Leah smiled and nodded her consent. Mikah carefully lifted his son and cradled him in his arms. "Evanh is nice. But I would like to name him Arenh," he said.

"Arenh of Crimson Clan," Leah smiled. "I like that better than Evanh. And I think Arenh of Indigo Clan would like it too."

Mikah felt the thoughts and feelings of the Dreamers flowing through his mind. And among them was a new stream of thought—and yet it was familiar—a current of feelings with which he was intimately acquainted. "Yes," he smiled, "Lord Arenh of the Indigo Clan likes it very much."

Mikah looked down at the baby in his arms, who had fallen fast asleep. "My dear sweet Arenh," he said. And though Leah didn't realize it at the time, Mikah was now speaking to Arenh of the Indigo Clan, "May all your dreams be sweet, my love."

Chapter 25—Back in the garden

FOR JUST an instant, everything was clear. Arenh understood it all. He could see the entire planet from here, a tiny green and blue marble of a world, almost lost in the vastness of the blackness around it. Then he woke up with a start as the tones of the garden chime filled the morning air around the upper entrance to the Mountain.

He had spent the night in the stone watchtower at the edge of the terrace. The cot in the tower wasn't as comfortable as his bed in the Carnelian Cavern, but it was adequate. And the view from the watchtower was magnificent in the morning.

He got up and stood at the door of the tower, stretching for a moment as he breathed in the foggy air, heavy with the fragrance of the honeysuckles that covered the fences. His garden bot was already busy watering the supersoy seedlings they had planted the day before.

A red and blue butterfly fluttered across the garden and settled on his shoulder. "*Such a beautiful morning,*" it whispered in his ear. ...